CONDOR ONE

John Simpson

Dreamspinner Press

Published by
Dreamspinner Press
4760 Preston Road
Suite 244-149
Frisco, TX 75034
http://www.dreamspinnerpress.com/

Cover Art by Dan Skinner/Cerberus Inc. cerberusinc@hotmail.com
Cover Design by Mara McKennen

ISBN: 978-0-9817372-8-7

Printed in the United States of America
First Edition
July, 2008

eBook edition available in Adobe PDF, MobiPocket and MS Reader formats.
eBook ISBN: 978-0-9817372-9-4

To my mother Ruth who has sacrificed much on my behalf during her life and who has had to put up with more injustice than any one person should ever have to endure in one life. On that certain final day, may she find justice and happiness in the company of her father Harry and all the Saints and Angels of heaven.

Authors Note

While this is a work of fiction, it reflects my imagination of what it would be like should any candidate for the Presidency of the United States be identified as being gay. In the world as it currently exists, much of our society runs on prejudice and hatred when it comes to the gay community. Chiefly this occurs, due to a lack of understanding of why some people are destined to be born gay, and the subsequent failure of teaching of tolerance for those who are different. May the evolution of the human race consign this problem to the dust heap of history where racial prejudice properly lies.

CHAPTER 1
HIGH DRAMA

It was six weeks until the general election for the President of the United States and the stakes could not be higher. The state of the world was tense with a fair certainty that nuclear weapons had been introduced into Syria by Russia, the newly emerged and reinvigorated American adversary. Israel was reacting as one might expect: with the panic of a state facing the threat of extinction. All over Tel Aviv little cars with military escorts darted like bees between flowers as they shuttled the General Flag officers from meeting to meeting. Iran and its close ally Iraq were rattling their sabers so loudly that no one in Washington was getting any sleep at night. Pizza delivery vehicles were seen making regular visits to the Pentagon, a sure sign that the midnight oil of the Military Industrial Complex was burning brightly. The entire Middle East was once again the tinderbox that threatened to ignite the whole world. In the United States, another kind of war was raging: the presidential election campaign of 2012. Democrat David J. Windsor, a multi-millionaire corporate executive, was running against Speaker of the House Daniel Gorski, the Republican nominee. Both candidates followed the norms of their parties, firing millions of dollars of attack ads at each other and dividing the nation in the process. Everyone was worried about who would answer that White House phone at three A.M.

Windsor came from a liberal background and was related to the royal family of England, where King William had just ascended to the throne after the death of Queen Elizabeth II. Prince Charles had declined the crown, clearing the way for William V to become King of England. Gorski was ever the conservative hawk who – while mouthing the rhetoric of smaller government, tighter budgets, and isolationism – practiced the exact opposites in a continued attempt to make America ruler of the world ... all at the expense of social programs and a decaying infrastructure that was well beyond becoming a *potential* danger to the American public. His social outlook was typical Republican fare: anti-gay, anti-women, and anti-minority, with a very strong dash of evangelicalism.

The Vice-Presidential candidates were wedded to the politics, philosophies, and priorities of their running-mates – or at least they professed to be. Windsor had chosen an older governor from the Deep South to help him carry that part of the country. Governor Barry Miller of Florida was thirty-five years Windsor's senior, but he wanted the job and had good skills. He added weight to the ticket in both age and experience.

The differences between the two candidates at the top of the tickets could not have been sharper, and this made most pundits agree that the nation's choice was clear. One was charting a course forward for the country; the other was promising the status quo legacy of the outgoing President, whose family had controlled the White House for twelve long, troubled years. The final debate of the campaign was due to begin shortly and had the full attention of the American public. The setting was the University of Central Florida, near Orlando, Florida. Once again, it all came down to Florida.

"DAVID, we need to get going to the debate if we are going to be on time; it's about a fourteen-minute ride out to the University," advised sixty-four year old Mary, my longtime Secretary.

"Yeah, okay. Let's get going. Two minutes."

As the motorcade whisked along from downtown Orlando to the debate site, my mind wandered over the last six months of what was more than a slightly caustic campaign. The far right was determined to keep the White House in their column and the Democratic Party was determined to recapture the people's house after a very long twelve years of near dictatorial rule. If I were to become President, I would reverse many of the policies that had strangled the American people over the last decade – no more conservative buffoons on the Supreme Court while I was President.

"David, here are your note cards with every position that the campaign has taken since it began. We don't know what Gorski is going to throw at you tonight, but they feel their edge on you slipping away, so they may be desperate enough to try and create a controversy that they can ride until Election Day," Mary said.

"Thanks, Mary. I'm going to try and just be me – give the people one last chance to see me for who I really am. I'm asking for their trust, as well as their vote. I want to be as forthright as I can be – contrast that with Gorski's obvious spin. People are tired of that kind of 'politics-as-usual.' This is it: the final debate, and the final chance for America to see both of us together. I really hope that the people will get a good look at the polar opposites that are vying for the White House."

As the motorcade came to a halt outside the side entrance to the University auditorium, car doors flung open and Secret Service agents emerged from the various SUV's that were a part of modern day security, taking up their 'ground' positions ready for the candidate to exit the limousine. I sat in the back waiting for the signal from the agent at the door, Shane Thompson, that it was okay to exit the vehicle. I watched the final radio check, the agent finally opening my door so I could get out. A large crowd had gathered outside the auditorium, unable to get into the event since all available seats were already taken. I waved to the crowd as the security agents whisked me into the side entrance and escorted to me to a holding room where we would wait until the time drew near for the debate to begin. This way, my exposure to unforeseen circumstances was kept to a minimum. I had been advised that the crowd was not only large, but also friendly and about evenly divided between Gorski and me. I took the last few moments to go over my note cards for the final time as makeup people worked on my face and hair.

"Mr. Windsor, it's 7:55, we should move to the launch position for the stage, sir," advised Agent Alvarez, the agent in charge of my security detail.

"Okay, let's get the show going."

We quickly moved from the holding room to the left side of the stage and waited the final moments behind the curtains. The Secret Service for both candidates scanned the crowd one final time before both of us were exposed on stage. At exactly 8:00 P.M., I heard Anderson Cooper from CNN begin the announcement to the television audience that the debate was about to begin. Speaker Gorski was introduced first, and he came out from the opposite side of the stage to applause and took his seat. Next, I heard my name, and I moved out on stage and took my seat, smiling and waving to the crowd as the applause this time was for me. The red lights of the television cameras told me that they were on and showing us to the world. The final debate was scheduled to last ninety minutes, using the standard format from all our previous debates.

Our biggest policy disagreement was on foreign relations and how to deal with the situation in Syria. Gorski wanted a relationship that was confrontational while I wanted to seek diplomatic solutions to our problems if at all possible. I was not afraid to use our military might, but it was going to be my last choice if necessary. There really were no surprises or sucker punches and I was feeling that the debate was not truly a win for either Gorski or me until the final fifteen minutes.

"SPEAKER GORSKI, we are in our final quarter hour of the debate and you may address any issue that remains," invited Cooper.

"Thank you, Anderson. There is one final issue that I think the American people need to be aware of as, it may affect their decision as to whom to vote for as their President. Certain information has come to light about the personal life of Mr. Windsor and I would like a response to this information from him. Mr. Windsor, are you or are you not a homosexual?"

The auditorium went deadly quiet as people tried to understand the question that was just asked of the Democratic candidate for President. Had they heard correctly? Had the Speaker of the U.S. House of Representatives just asked his opponent if he was gay? After a moment of total silence, multiple flashes occurred as the print media began to take photograph after photograph of the situation unfolding before the eyes of the world.

"Mr. Gorski, may I ask what relevance my sexuality has to do with the job of President of the United States? What is your purpose in asking such a question?"

"Mr. Windsor, the American people have the right to know if their President sleeps with men and if he violates the tenets of the Bible that we all hold so dear as we were founded as a Christian nation. As for my purpose in asking, it is to expose the truth about who you really are as a man."

"Gentlemen, I don't think that is a proper question to be asked during this debate and I would suggest to you, Mr. Windsor, that you not answer this question," said Anderson.

Part of the audience began to clap in agreement, while others began to murmur.

"Thank you, Anderson, but I fully intend to answer the question. Let us be clear about the intent of the Speaker in asking this question. He hopes to make me run and hide, to be embarrassed, to cripple me in the closing days of the election since he cannot win on the issues facing this great nation. He expects me to lie, to try and evade the question and to attack him for asking it. He is wrong on all counts. Ladies and Gentlemen, in fact, I am a gay American. I have been gay all my life, and will always be gay. This fact has absolutely nothing to do with my abilities to be the best President you possibly could have, leading the American people out of the darkness that has been characterized by just such a question. It is the politics of fear, hatred and bigotry, and I soundly reject it. My being gay will have no effect whatsoever on how I conduct the affairs of state. I will represent the American people and their interests with pride, competence, and honesty, and I promise to never lie to the people of this great country. Finally, Mr. Gorski is also wrong as usual about this nation being founded as a Christian nation. It was not. The founding fathers were in fact Deists, and not Christians. In fact, if you read the words of Thomas Jefferson, you will find that he had a particular distaste for

Christianity. As for the ministers and preachers that Mr. Gorski so favors, Jefferson had this to say: 'In every country and in every age, the priest has been hostile to liberty. He is always in alliance with the despot, abetting his abuses in return for protection to his own.' – Thomas Jefferson to Horatio G. Spafford, in 1814."

The applause was deafening. People rose to their feet and continued to clap and began to chant my name over and over again. Gorski looked as though he had eaten a rotten egg and was in shock at the opposite response his question brought about rather than the one anticipated. Anderson tried to bring the crowd under control but it took him over two minutes to regain control of the auditorium.

"Mr. Windsor, how do you think the evangelical vote will view this stunning revelation?"

"First of all, Anderson, I never had the evangelical vote to begin with, so in fact I lose nothing by being honest with the people. Second, those who consider themselves Christians will remember that the greatest commandment given to us by Jesus was to love one another and to love God. In fact, Jesus never said anything about being gay. So, if my being honest on this topic gives them pause, then I suggest that they examine the true pillars of their faith and go from there. I will not pander to the religious right in order to get elected. I leave that in the capable hands of the Speaker of the House."

"Now just a damn minute here...."

"I'm sorry, Mr. Speaker, but we are out of time, and I thank you for being here with us this evening on what has turned out to be an historic debate. Thank you and good night."

Once again, the crowd broke out in applause and began to chant my name. This did not please Gorski, who turned red and instead of offering the traditional handshake at the end of the debate, he simply walked off the stage. I moved forward and shook Anderson's hand and thanked him for moderating the debate.

"Mr. Windsor, it's going to be an interesting few weeks until the election, and I wish you good luck, sir."

"Thank you, Anderson, and I hope to see you again."

Waving to the crowd, I walked off the stage towards my group of people. The Secret Service detail actually came out on stage to meet me part way and escorted me off stage. Before I could really discuss anything about what had just happened, the Secret Service moved me quickly out of the auditorium and into the motorcade, which had already started their engines and were prepared to quickly move out once we were aboard. The sirens wailed and we took off at a fairly fast pace, leaving the University of Central Florida faster than we had arrived. The Secret Service was anxious and it showed.

"Mr. Windsor, can we have a few moments to speak when we get to the hotel?" asked Alvarez.

"Of course we can, just give me a couple of minutes to get relaxed and grab a diet 7-up."

Mary turned her head to me and said, "Well, that cat's out of the bag now, isn't it? I wonder how long it took them to come up with that information to ambush you with tonight."

"Oh, I imagine they've had it all along and only used it tonight because they fear they're losing this election. Gorski sure was pissed at the response from the audience, wasn't he?" I asked with a laugh.

"We knew this night might come. Now we have to see how it affects your poll numbers in the morning. The talk shows will be screaming tonight over this, you wait and see."

Arriving at the Hilton resort in Orlando, the security team did the usual things, and I got out of the limo and headed into the hotel. The press was everywhere shouting questions at me about the fact that I was gay, and wanting more information. I just ignored them and kept walking, having no intention of stoking the fires any more tonight. The Secret Service was able to keep the reporters far from me, and we glided into the elevator to ride to the top floor where we arrived at their version of the Presidential suite.

We entered the suite to the sound of ringing telephones and a stack of messages that had come in since the revelation on television. I waved them all off and headed into the main bedroom so that I could take off my jacket and tie. Wiping my face with a cold wet washcloth immediately brought back some needed energy.

When I came out of the bedroom, Mary handed me my soda and I took a seat in the living room area of the suite. I motioned to Agent Alvarez to come over, and told him to sit down. While the low-level hum of business carried on, I asked Alvarez what was on his mind.

"In light of the information that you confirmed this evening, our job of protecting you might have just gotten a little bit harder. There are more than a few nut jobs and groups in this country who are going to go ballistic because you've admitted that you're gay."

"I realize that, but what would you have me do? Take a pill and become straight? It doesn't happen that way, Agent Alvarez, and if it did, I wouldn't take the pill. I'm quite comfortable being who I am."

"No, sir, I didn't mean it that way. I just meant that we're going to have to tighten your security even more when you are in public, especially the close-in security. Those agents will be at your side now all the time."

"I understand and can accept that. I like Agent Thompson; he seems like a really nice guy. Is he good at his job?"

"Yes sir, all the agents are good at their job or they wouldn't be on this detail."

"Fine, then I'd like Thompson assigned as close-in security."

"I see no problem with that sir, I'll notify him, and his new duties will begin in the morning. He'll have to keep the same schedule that you do, so if you could make sure that I always have an updated copy of your agenda, it will make it a lot easier."

"Fine, just see Mary any time you need an update. Now, let me be frank with you, Agent Alvarez. Do you believe that any of the agents, including yourself, will want to be taken off this detail now that you all know that I am gay?"

"Mr. Windsor, the fact that you are gay does not change the fact that you are the nominee of one of the two political parties of the

United States and may in fact become President. This changes nothing, sir."

The meeting over, I turned my attention to the message stack that had now grown to one hundred and twenty four since my departure for the debate.

CHAPTER 2
THE BOOK OF REVELATIONS

Many of the messages I held in my hand were from big donors to the campaign; all worried that I had shot myself in the foot by admitting I was gay. One message simply said, "Couldn't you have waited until after the election to discuss your personal life?" It seemed they overlooked one thing: the other guy brought out the fact that I was gay; I didn't just volunteer the information. Of course, there had been rumors all during the campaign that I was gay since there was a total lack of evidence of any romantic connection to women in my life. I was never one to pretend to be straight by using a 'beard' as they used to say in Hollywood. This of course didn't mean that I never went out socially with friends who happened to be female. But the Republican attack dogs had their red meat, and now we would see what they were going to do with it.

Going to bed after talking with my staff, I replayed the conversation with the Agent Alvarez. I was pleased that he had agreed to allow Special Agent Thompson to become one of my close-in protectors. Thompson was a young agent, in his late twenties, tall, over six feet, about two hundred pounds, blonde hair and green eyes. He appeared well built as all the agents did, and his stunning looks had caught my eye when he joined the detail. He was very professional, always called me sir, or Mr. Windsor, and was an extreme delight to be around. I might actually enjoy this part of my security.

I woke up at 6:45 A.M., showered and dressed and sat down on the sofa while an aide poured coffee and orange juice and handed me a stack of papers, both local and national. Of course the lead headline without exception was the fact that the Democrat who had won the nomination for the election was a homosexual. The flavor of the accompanying stories went from amazement that bordered on glee from the New York Times, to announcements that the world was about to end from the Manchester Union Leader in New Hampshire. Just as in politics, the papers voiced opinions that jelled with their political and social philosophy. It was as I had expected.

"Good morning, David, did you sleep well last night?" Mary asked.

"Once I got to sleep, yes, I never woke up until this morning. Would you return these phone calls, and simply reassure the people that I am the same person they have supported all along, and that the fact that I am now known as a gay man doesn't change a thing? Tell them I am working hard to win the White House as I have been doing for fourteen months now."

"Of course, I'll handle these before we leave for the airport in ninety minutes."

Secret Service answered a knock on the door, revealing the morning courier with my overnight intelligence briefing, which both candidates for the White House received each morning so that we could stay on top of world affairs and talk intelligently about the issues. After all, either Gorski or I would be sitting in the Oval Office in just over three months, and whoever it was would be commander in chief. I had a second cup of coffee while I quickly reviewed the report and noted that there had been no easing of tensions in the Middle East, and that Russia was still trying to keep the pressure up on Israel to make concessions involving inspections of their supposed nuclear weapons. This of course, would never happen. This was merely a ploy by the Russians to build up influence in the region and secure their much-needed source of oil. In another part of the world, Chavez of Venezuela was threatening war with his neighbor Columbia. I considered Chavez one of the more dangerous persons in South America because he believed his own propaganda.

I finished my coffee, handed the briefing book to Mary, and got my jacket on. My suitcase had been packed for me, and we were ready to leave for the airport. Special Agent Thompson, looking very handsome in the morning sunlight, asked if we were ready to go.

"I'm all set, lead the way, Agent."

Thompson spoke into his hand mic, "Condor is on the move," and out the door we went and into the motorcade to the airport. It took only another ten minutes and we were aboard the chartered aircraft and settling in for the next stop on the campaign.

After we were airborne, I asked Mary to call a meeting in the front of the aircraft with my closest aides. The topic would be how the campaign would change now that the fact that I was gay had been publicized.

"Okay, people, we have an entirely new campaign in front of us in the closing weeks. Gorski thinks he scored a touchdown by outing me to the American people last night. It's going to be your jobs to handle the flack that we get from the revelation. John, schedule a meeting with the gay leadership council, the ones we met with about four months ago. We are going to need every bit of their support now. Make it for this Saturday in Washington."

"How long do you think we'll need?"

"Better make it for two hours and ask them to have their PR people there along with their field coordinators. Sam, you prepare a statement that we'll all use about my love life. I have no one special in my life; I'm not seeing anyone, and I have been too busy running for President to even have time for much of a personal life. This should eliminate any furtive questions about who sleeps in my bed. Count on the Republican smear machine to try and dig up every guy I have ever slept with and try and get a statement from them. Fortunately, my past boyfriends are all still friends, and I know I can count on them to be discreet. Besides, I'm sure they will all want an invite to the White House if I'm elected, and that is way more important to them than five minutes of fame from some newspaper story."

"How do you want to handle any probing questions on how long you've been gay, and that sort of inquiry?" asked Mary.

"I do not want to hide or run from this thing. We tell the people the truth, as much of it as they are entitled to. They don't have the right to know what I do in bed, but they do have the right to know that it is with men. I felt no need to bring it up before as it is not germane to the job of President, but since the opposition has brought it to light, we face it head on. No lies."

"Understood, Dave," replied Mary.

"Now as luck would have it, our next campaign stop is back in California, specifically San Francisco. So, we should get a good reception today and at least have a one-day delay in the attacks that are coming. There shouldn't be any protesters. Sam, schedule a stop in the Castro. We might as well embrace this thing. Eddie, write up a few comments that I can make if there is an opportunity to speak; maybe two paragraphs, but make them policy type comments. Anything else we need to discuss?"

"A real interesting piece of information here, Dave: overnight, we raised a little over one million dollars over the Internet in new campaign donations. It's money we can put directly into the battleground states on television ads the week before the election."

"You're kidding? The Republicans blast us with the gay thing and we bring in a million bucks because of it? Any idea where the money came from?"

"I'm told it's mostly small donations from new donors spread across the country. Sixty-four percent were from males, the remainder from females. It could be the gay community, or it could be people who now believe in you as the first totally honest candidate for President to come along since Roosevelt."

"Okay, give me a daily report from now on regarding internet donations for the preceding twenty four hour period. Anything else? Okay, let's break and work on the stuff for the rest of this week."

Everyone went back to their seats and Mary handed me a cup of coffee, smiling and telling me things would be all right. That maybe, just maybe, Gorski did us a favor. After all, I would no longer have to hide the fact that I was gay.

As she walked away, I saw Agent Thompson looking at me and look away quickly when I noticed him. I motioned for Thompson to come over and sit down next to me.

"I just wanted to say, Agent Thompson, that if you are uncomfortable being close-in for me because I'm gay, I'd like you to tell me so I can pick another agent to take those duties over for you. I don't want you to have anything on your mind but your job."

"No sir, not at all. I'm very comfortable with this assignment. In fact, sir, I'm proud of you in many respects."

"Proud of me? For what?"

"You could have danced all around the revelation last night, but you didn't. You handled it with honesty and pride and I respect you very much for that. You could lose the race for being honest. It's not something the Service is used to seeing: a politician who is honest and above board. I'm very pleased to be your close-in agent, sir, and I consider it an honor."

"Thank you; I really don't know what to say to that, Agent. I promised myself a long time ago when I decided to run for President that I would not lie to the American people unless it was a matter of national security and for their well being. You know, you're probably going have much longer hours now with these duties than you did before – don't you have a wife or girlfriend who is going to be upset with you over that?"

"No sir, I'm single and unattached. It may sound corny, sir, but the Secret Service is my partner."

"Well, Agent, don't waste your youth without the love of that special person in your life. A career is fine to be married to, but it makes for a cold bed on a winter night. And frankly, Agent Alvarez looks like a tough wife to have looking over your shoulder all the time," I said with a laugh.

"Yes sir, you have no idea!"

As Thompson got up and walked away, I couldn't help but wonder what he looked like out of his suit. He reminded me of a young

Brad Pitt, and his hair was incredible. Damn, I couldn't even check out his ass; his suit jacket hung down too low. I chided myself for that thought. Now was not the time to be thinking of Thompson in that way.

I handled several calls from worried main-line contributors who were bundlers, assuring them that the race was not lost because I was gay. I understood that these people worked very hard to gather up donations from many different people and then bundle them up and send them into the campaign. The 2012 Presidential campaign was projected to cost in excess of one billion dollars, the highest in campaign history. There simply was nothing I could do about the fact that Gorski had outed me, at least not until I became President. After reading more briefing papers on our campaigns' various positions, I took a nap in order to look my best in San Francisco.

IT was six weeks since we landed in San Francisco to what turned out to be a triumphant campaign stop that solidified our support in California. It was election night 2011, and we along with the rest of the world were glued to our television screens. The Windsor party was in the Presidential suite at the Waldorf Astoria in New York City. The polls had us dead even with Gorski, with projections that went both ways. No one knew who was going to be the next President until the votes were counted, and it was one hour exactly until the East Coast polls closed and the first results would come in.

Over the previous six weeks, Gorski and the Republican Party tried their best to paint me as everything from the devil to a sex maniac. They made dire predictions that if I was elected President, Western Civilization would collapse and communism would finally win. Some even predicted that the Roman Catholic Church would implode, signaling the beginning of the end of mankind as foretold by Nostradamus. If it had not been so sad, it would have been funny.

As I looked around the suite, I saw that those closest to me in this world were with me. My mother, who had endured the terrible accusations in the press over the revelation of my sexuality, was here; my campaign management team, which in my opinion was the finest in

the world; two secret Service Agents, one of whom was Agent
Thompson; and a couple of hotel wait staff serving everybody snacks
and drinks. I was again admiring Thompson who looked stunning this
evening in his black suit, white shirt, blue tie, and beautiful blonde hair.
He still reminded me very much of a young Brad Pitt, with that brilliant
blonde hair the color of straw. He smiled at me when he saw me
looking him over and I nodded my head to him and smiled back. I
wonder if he knew how hot I found him. True to his word, he never
left my side the entire time he was my close-in agent, and we had come
to know each other well in that short time. I also noticed that Alvarez
had barked at him on several occasions, for nothing more than being
with me all the time. I detected a note of jealousy in Alvarez over the
situation, and I was keeping an eye on things.

Walking over to where Thompson was standing, I asked him if
he would like to sit down with me and watch the returns.

"Ah, thank you, sir, but that would be against our post orders,
and if Alvarez caught me sitting down with the principle, I would be
chasing counterfeiters on Guam within a week."

"Well, I don't want you to get into any trouble, but you don't
have to worry about ever being assigned to Guam, I'll see to that."

"Thank you, sir, I appreciate that," he replied with a smile, the
smile that made my knees go weak.

"If I am elected President tonight, will you be able to spend
some off duty time with me, just to chat? Sure, I have a lot of people
around talking to me all the time, but you are someone I would enjoy
getting to know better."

"That would be possible, sir. I voted for you, by the way; of
course we're not supposed to talk about that with anyone."

"Well, thank you, you have good judgment."

We smiled at each other and stared into each other's eyes just a
moment longer than usual. I was beginning to think that Thompson
might be gay. Could I be that lucky?

"If I have a victory speech to give tonight, stay close to me, will you?"

"Sir, is there a problem that we need to know about? Is there a threat?"

"No, no, nothing like that. I'd just like you to be near tonight. There will be a lot of emotion flowing freely from many people and I need to count on you to keep me from getting overwhelmed."

"Of course, sir, that goes without saying."

"Very well then, nothing to do but wait for the returns," I said as I turned and walked back to the sofa and rejoined my campaign people.

It took over six hours for all the returns to come in, and it wasn't until two A.M. that a winner of the entire race could be called: I was to be the next President of the United States, thanks to the good people of Washington State who put me over the top. As the declaration by the media swept over the room, all hell broke loose in a cacophony of celebration. We almost didn't hear the phone ring when it did. We got the room calmed down, as Mary came in from another room, and announced that it was Gorski on the phone. I assumed it was his concession notification to me.

"Hello, Mr. Speaker."

"Hello, Mr. Windsor, I'm calling to congratulate you on your victory and to formally concede the election to you. I don't know how you did it, frankly, with your being gay revealed to the world, and I think you are going to be tested severely in more than just a few ways. My advice to you is to surround yourself with good advisors; you're going to need them."

"Thank you, Mr. Speaker, for your good wishes and concession. Never underestimate the American people, for when you do, they will do something that will surprise you every time, like electing me President. If you will excuse me now, I have a speech to give."

I hung up the phone and reflected for a moment on the sadness and slight bitter tinge to Gorski's words. I would not have wanted to make that concession call either and I'm sure he was glad that it was over. Losing to a gay man must have made it all the more difficult for his own ego to accept. Mary advising me that Agent Alvarez wanted to see me interrupted my thoughts.

"Okay, Mary, tell him to come in, and tell everyone else we are leaving for the ballroom downstairs where I will make my victory speech."

"Yes, Mr. President."

With those three words, the immensity of the situation struck me like a thunderbolt. In just a little over two months, I would be the President of the United States.

"Congratulations on your victory, President-elect Windsor."

"Thank you, Agent Alvarez, we'll be going down to the ballroom shortly to make the victory speech. What can I do for you?"

"Well, sir, now that you are officially the next President, there will be some changes that you will notice. First, your security detail will increase by ten men everywhere you go, with an advance team doubled in size. The regular Presidential detail will be replacing all of the agents that have been with you during the campaign. Your present agents will be assigned support duties or assigned to a different area altogether. Your motorcade will now include an additional two 'battle wagons,' and you will be given a new limousine that will have advanced communication gear on board, and is up-armored even more than the limo you have been using. The police escort will be increased, and all personnel that come in daily contact with you will be required to have a full background investigation and clearances for the White House. Any questions, sir?"

"Not so much a question as a request. I would like Agent Thompson to remain with me as my personal bodyguard."

"Sir, I'm not sure that's possible. Agent Thompson doesn't have the advanced training required of the White House detail, and it's normal procedure to change out the team."

"Then schedule Agent Thompson for the necessary further training. I want him with me, is that clear, or do I have to call the Director?"

"No, sir, that won't be necessary. I'll have to inform the Secret Service Director of this departure from normal procedures, however. He has the final say on the matter."

"Actually, I have the final say in this particular matter. Shall we head on down to the ballroom?"

"Of course, sir, the team will be in the hallway waiting."

"Okay, Mary, is everyone ready?"

"Yes, sir, I'll call down to the reception area and let them know you're coming so they can advise the networks. I'll remain here, answer the phones and watch you on the TV."

Opening the door to the suite, I found a dozen agents waiting for me and we headed towards the elevators. We got into two elevators that were being held for us and were whisked non-stop to the ballroom on the second floor. When the doors opened, another group of agents and police officers were waiting to escort me to the waiting area of the ballroom. The noise was deafening, the crowd in full celebration mode, and it took another five minutes to get everyone calmed down so that the Congressman who was going to introduce me could speak. When the noise level settled to reasonable, I moved to the edge of the stage platform behind the curtains.

"Ladies and gentlemen, it is my extreme pleasure and honor to introduce to you the next President of the United States, David Windsor!"

The crowd erupted once again into a chaotic celebration as I walked out onto the stage, waving at the crowd and television cameras. Balloons rained down from the ceiling like snowflakes at the North Pole. The ballroom was packed, two thousand people, all-pushing forward waving and hollering. I looked around for Agent Thompson who was very much a security blanket for me. I found him standing down on the floor directly in front and slightly to the left of the podium.

Anyone rushing the stage head-on would run into Thompson and three other agents standing in front of me.

I continued to wave at the crowd and smile as the band played 'Happy Days are Here Again' with gusto. It took another ten minutes to get the crowd quiet enough to begin speaking.

"I am pleased to inform you that a short time ago, Mr. Gorski telephoned and conceded the election to me." Once again, the crowd roared their approval and another five minutes passed before I could continue.

"Tonight is an historic occasion, a night in which the Democratic Party has reclaimed the White House after a long dark period in American history. As I said to you on the campaign trail, I will never lie to you, never mislead you, and always work for you!"

Once more the crowd roared with approval.

"Tomorrow is a new beginning, a beginning for the rebirth of America, an America that you can be proud of around the world. I intend to restore the dignity, honor, and democratic leadership that America has been known for in the past, and will once again be known for in the future. Together we can move this country forward so that our social programs can meet the needs of those who need them the most while maintaining our national security. I pledge to you tonight that I will never use the American military without just reason, and after full consultation with the representatives of the people who labor in Congress. To the friends of America, know that our friendship will continue as long as you treat your citizens with dignity in full recognition of their human rights. To our enemies, a special message: Do not misunderstand or underestimate me because I am a gay man, for before all other things, I am first an American and the President of the United States. If forced to, I will not hesitate to use American military might in the face of aggression or endangerment of the interests of the United States."

The crowd went absolutely wild over this statement. As I'd hoped, this part of my speech laid to rest many fears of those who were concerned that a gay man would not be a strong leader in military affairs, and that he might reduce the image of the United States. The public had a lot to learn about who David Windsor was, and would be as President.

"And so, my fellow Americans, you who have placed your trust in me will not be disappointed. In the days to come you will hear who I am choosing for my cabinet, and other important positions in my Administration. I invite you to walk with me as we go forward and make this great nation what it should be. Thank you and God bless you all."

I continued to wave at the crowd and shake hands with those on stage as cameras recorded the event for posterity. Finally, I left the stage, meeting the heavy security presence, which swiftly took me back up to what was now the Presidential suite.

AT that moment in a different part of the country, six shadowy men threw invectives at the television screen. They were not pleased by either my election or my victory speech.

"It's a sad day for America when the President of this nation is a homosexual. He's an embarrassment, but as happened before with JFK, we can once again correct a mistake made by the voters. We will 'unelect' this man and remove him from the White House for good," said the man in charge.

"But who will be our Oswald?" asked another in the room as he took a sip of Scotch.

"One thing's for sure, we have no shortage of willing and able Oswalds. We'll leave that issue up to the mechanics of the operation. After all, that's why they get a lot of money from us each year."

CHAPTER 3
THE TRANSITION

As late November came and a strong chill took to the air for the rest of the winter, my people opened an office in Washington, D.C. known as 'The Transition Office'. This taxpayer-funded office and staff's sole job was to transition Administrations, so that an orderly transfer of power would take place as envisioned in the Constitution. The Windsor Transition Office was located on K Street in D.C. in the heart of lobbyist territory. Very competent people undertook the urgent task of selecting and vetting personnel to fill key roles in the Administration who had to be on the job on day one. Lists of names were scanned over as credentials were checked and double-checked. This had to be done not only for the Office of the President, but also the Office of the Vice-President. Liaisons were set up between the current White House and the Transition Office, which was supposed to be a cooperative process between all parties. This did not happen, as the current Administration made what the out-going Clinton Administration did look like child's play – which it was. To remove the letter W from all computers and typewriters was a juvenile prank played on the Bush Administration. However, there was no active obstructionism between the Clinton and Bush teams as there was now. Clearances that had to be processed by the White House to the FBI were often delayed, making it hard for the team to do its job. The opposition party was going to make it as difficult as possible for the incoming Administration. What was worse, they were proud of the trouble they were creating. After receiving a call in Colorado where I was on vacation, advising me of the problems, I decided to fly to Washington, and meet with the President. This problem needed to be ended, and ended now. When a phone call was placed to the White House to arrange to meet with the sitting President, his schedule was full, or so I was told. I was now getting as mad as my staff was at how immature these people were behaving.

As my motorcade reached the Transition Office, I was told that the President would see me – on January 20th. I got out of the car so fast that the Secret Service had trouble keeping up with me as I stormed into the offices of the transition team.

"Donald, tell me what the latest situation is with the White House."

"Sir, all of our current choices for staff positions and cabinet posts have yet to be sent to the FBI. I'm worried that by the time we get them there, we'll be taking office without having any staff with security clearances, which will make them unable to function properly."

"We'll see about that. Mary, get me the Director of the FBI on the phone, please."

"Yes, Mr. President."

I slammed my office door even though I didn't mean to. It got everyone's attention in the office. Agent Thompson took up his post immediately outside my door.

"Director Mendelssohn on line one, sir."

"Director Mendelssohn, President-elect Windsor here, how are you?"

"I'm doing all right, sir, what can I do for you?"

"I'm going to be straightforward with you, Director. The current White House will not pass onto your office for clearance any of the people chosen to serve in my administration. As you know, they cannot legally come into contact with classified material without that clearance. I need your help."

"Mr. Windsor, you know the protocol for this: selections have to be forwarded to my office through the White House and I really can't change that procedure. I'm afraid I can't do anything for you."

"Well, maybe you can advise me on something that has been weighing on my mind."

"Of course, sir, if there is anything I can answer for you, I'd be happy to."

"Great. How long does it take to clear someone for the position of FBI Director?"

"Sir? I don't need any other clearances than the ones I already have."

"On January 20th, at 12:01 P.M., you will no longer be FBI Director, and your replacement will need his security clearances, and I want them in place."

"You're replacing me? I still have three years left on my term as Director!"

"You, sir, serve at the pleasure of the President, and your continuation in the Director's office does not serve me well. Therefore, I will nominate my own Director."

"Ah, Mr. President, if I were able to assist you with all that you currently need, would that change your mind?"

"Of course. I don't like to get rid of experienced men if I don't have to. Politics has no role in the FBI, don't you agree?"

"Why, absolutely, sir. Just have your secretary, I believe her name is Mary Nixon, send over the clearance file, and I'll have agents begin working on it at once."

"Outstanding, I'm glad you could see this my way."

I hung up by punching the intercom button and telling Mary to send over the file to the Director's office personally. There was more than one way to get around roadblocks in Washington. It was time for a meeting with top staff.

"Okay, everyone listen up. We work around the White House for whatever we need. That bunch of clowns will no longer delay the important work that has to be done in just a few short weeks. Daniel, if you have any further problems, let me know at once. The security clearances will be worked on by the FBI starting today – end of that problem. What else has been held up?"

"No one has been able to get into the White House to measure spaces or inspect the private residence that you will be using to determine if you want any changes made."

"Call Bill Clinton's people and see if they still have all the measurements that you need. As for my quarters, I can wait until we throw them out on Pennsylvania Avenue for any decorating. I'm sure the residence has been done in 'early tacky' and will have to be redone. Daniel, see to it that a story is leaked to the press about this hostile environment that has been created by the White House and how it is hindering the orderly process of changing administrations. Anything else, any other delays?"

"No, sir, that would help us out a lot to be able to get these things done," replied Daniel.

"Good. Okay, everyone get to work, we have an administration to form!"

After everyone left, Agent Thompson knocked on the door. I motioned for him to come in, knowing he could see me through the office window. I needed something pleasant to deal with at the moment.

"Excuse me, sir, may I speak with you?"

"Of course, what is it, Shane?"

That was the first time I'd used his first name and he smiled and then quickly got back to business.

"Sir, I can't help but hear almost everything that goes on, and I know you're having problems with the White House. A couple of my buddies on the White House detail have told me that they've heard the current President ordering staff to be uncooperative with you and your team. I just thought you might like to know that."

"Well, that confirms what I already suspected. Let them enjoy themselves while they can, because very soon they'll be out of the corridors of power. By the way, Shane, I'm not sure if you know. I've requested that you stay with me as my close-in security once I'm President. I've told Alvarez and after initial objections about advanced training, I told him to get you that training and that I expected to see you by my side often."

"Sir, that jumps me over many agents who are senior to me, not to mention the entire White House detail. There's sure to be resistance from a number of people to such a move. But please know that I am honored that you made the request."

"Shane, I don't intend to let too many people tell me what I can and can't do. That includes requesting you, unless you personally object to the assignment."

"No, sir, I don't object at all. Usually you have to be in the protection division at least ten years to get assigned to the President. There will be some noses out of joint over this."

"Do you care?"

"Well, sir, to be honest, no," Shane answered with a broad grin.

"Then it's settled, you'll be spending a lot of time with me."

"I very much look forward to it, sir, and by the way, I would take a bullet for you if you've ever wondered."

"Good God, let's hope it never comes to that! Speaking of such unpleasant things, though, why don't you get the required advanced training so that you'll be ready for when I am sworn in? How long does that take?"

"That training lasts six weeks, but there isn't another class scheduled until June of 2012."

"Mary, get me the Director of the Secret Service, please," I spoke into the intercom. "Let me see if we can't get you trained especially for me."

"Sir, Director Stevens on line two."

"Director Stevens, David Windsor here, how are you?"

"Fine, sir, what can I do for you?"

"I'm not sure if you've been told of a special request that I have made of the Service, but I wish to have Special Agent Thompson assigned to me as close-in security once I'm President. I understand that six weeks of additional training are required to serve on the White House detail, is that correct?"

"Yes, Mr. Windsor, all agents must have this training to be qualified for the Presidential detail. You do know that Agent Thompson is a fairly new agent, don't you, and this isn't something that I would normally recommend?"

"Yes, I'm aware that the agent in question is fairly new, but I trust him totally, I'm comfortable around him, and since the agent in that position is someone who is with me much of the time, he's the one I prefer. Is that a problem for you?"

"No, sir, I just wanted to make sure you were aware of Agent Thompson's background, that's all. I will see that he's temporarily replaced now so he can leave for Greenbelt Maryland, where that particular facility is located, for the required training."

"Outstanding, Director Stevens, I appreciate that."

"Sir, while I have you on the phone, we need to meet face to face if you have any questions about what life is going to be like for you as President as it relates to the Secret Service. We try to give you as much privacy as we can, however, it's our mandate under the law to protect you, and those designated by law and those further who you designate for protection, to carry out our duties. At times you may feel crowded, but sir, it's a reality of the times and your position."

"I understand, and I appreciate your willingness to cooperate with me in this first choice regarding Thompson. I don't anticipate asking for very many deviations in the routine procedures of the Service, as I appreciate the difficulty of the duties carried out by your office."

"Thank you, sir, and please call upon me any time you need something or have a question."

"I will. Have a good day, Director."

I wondered as I hung up whether Director Stevens had spoken with Mendelssohn, to have granted such speedy acquiescence to my request.

"Well, that's settled, Shane. I imagine you'll be sent to Greenbelt shortly. I'll look forward to your return. Remind them that I expect to have you back no later than inauguration day."

"Yes, Mr. President, thank you."

His jacket was a little shorter today and I could see some of his ass when he left the office. It looked quite stunning. I would have to make sure I went swimming when he came back, I thought with a smile.

As Christmas drew near, the FBI clearances started to come back to the Transition Office, and people were officially informed that they had the jobs that had been offered to them contingent upon successful security approval. It was the first concrete sign that my Administration was taking form. All but two of my cabinet nominations were now cleared and the remaining two were expected shortly as no problems had come up as of yet.

Shane had been gone now for four weeks and I found that I missed seeing him more than I expected. I took comfort in the fact that he would return to my side in another two weeks. I decided to spend Christmas quietly and out of the limelight with my immediate family on the island of St. Thomas. The press would be far less in evidence than they would if I remained in the continental United States.

I continued to receive telephone and in-person updates on our progress through the Christmas break and was told that all arrangements were completed for the Presidential Inaugural Balls. These would be interesting because the press was already speculating whether I would bring a male date to dance with, in keeping with the tradition that the new President dances at least one dance at each Ball. I decided that my mother would accompany me to all the Balls except the one being hosted by the GLBT community, to which I had accepted an invitation to make it one of the official Balls. Who knew who I might dance with at that one?

On January 2nd, 2012, I once again entered the Transition Office in Washington, D.C. There I was reunited with my entire team, many of whom had worked through the holidays. I would not forget these people once I was President. I called for a top staff meeting for eleven o'clock that morning.

"Good morning all, it's good to see you and I give you my thanks for all the hard work you've been doing since this office was formed. I hope you took time to be with your families over the holidays. I would now like a complete update on where we are since in nineteen days, I will be sworn in as the next President."

"We now have all clearances back that were requested in the first batch to the FBI. They have been falling all over themselves to get these done and in fact asked us if there's anything else they can do for us," advised Harvey Bell, my campaign manager. "I don't know what you said to them over there, but whatever it was, it worked."

"Let's just say that I can be persuasive when I have to be," I replied with a broad smile that relayed far more than my words.

"The Clinton people kept meticulous notes on the White House as far as measurements, furniture, and all the physical details. We got most of what we need from that information, including some idea about the private residence. We also have the right to borrow works of art from the National Museum of Art for use in the White House."

"Good, I want every painting changed out that has been in there with the exception of any paintings of former Democratic Presidents. Move the JFK portrait to the private residence area so that I see it every morning. It will remind me daily that there are enemies of democracy everywhere."

"I've made a note of that, sir, and will make sure it's moved before you come back from being sworn in," stated Mary. "Who do you want to select the art works from the Museum?"

"Ask Dr. Matlick of the Art department at Georgetown University to select appropriate paintings. He's a man I consider a friend and I respect his knowledge of art works. On a different topic, when will I have the inaugural schedule, Mary?"

"The final details are being put together as we speak, so I hope to have it to you by the end of today."

"Okay, great. Final topic on the subject of the Balls, how are the ticketing requests going? Are all the right people being asked to attend? Have there been any declinations of the invitation by people who normally would attend these things?"

"It's been hectic trying to make sure that everyone's request is being handled properly. There have been no declines, and in fact, we have been turning people away as the tickets are almost gone. You, sir, have twenty-five that you can use for anyone you like. Just let me know who to invite and I will take care of the rest."

"Okay, Mary, will do. By the way, everyone, I have asked Mary to be my secretary in the White House and she has accepted."

"Yes, so you all better behave yourselves or you won't get an appointment to see the President. You have to come through me to get to him," she said with a laugh as everyone clapped for her.

"Okay, that's it for now, everyone back to work," I said.

Two days later, I met with the entire Cabinet-to-be. It was the first important meeting that would begin the shaping of my Administration. Twelve men and women were now in the confirmation process in the United States Senate, which I hoped would be completed within the next few days. Since Congress was almost evenly split between the two parties, and the White House was in the hands of a Democrat, I anticipated no problems.

"Good morning, ladies and gentlemen. Welcome to the first formal formation meeting of the Windsor Administration. Each of you will play a vital part in the success or failure of our policy agenda and I'm counting on you all to do your very best. This Administration will not be known for either failure or quagmire as the outgoing Administration has come to be known. In addition to competency I expect total loyalty to our goals and to me. This does not mean that you can't have a difference of opinion from me, the Vice-President or my top advisors. I want to know when you do disagree, because divergent viewpoints on a topic can be a vital part of the decision making process. So, when I ask for your opinion or position on a particular issue, whether in private or in meetings, I expect you to give voice to your opinions and feelings. What I don't want and can't tolerate is public disagreement with the White House or other cabinet officers that only serves to show disunity among the government and gives comfort to our enemies. And believe me when I say we have enemies, both foreign and domestic. There are a lot of people who are in total shock that we won this election. When that shock wears off, expect a concerted effort to bring us down. You only have to look at what the Republicans did to Bill Clinton for the entire time he was in the White House. Imagine what he could have accomplished had he not been sidelined by almost constant investigations by someone for something – most of which should have been left between Bill and his wife. If we're attacked for pure partisan political reasons, expect me to fight back hard. If, on the other hand, we've screwed up and the attack is justified, then I expect us to correct the situation so that we can quickly move forward. Each of you will head an executive department of the Government. You have agreed to take on grave responsibilities that could include being in the line of succession to take over as President should both I and the Vice-President not be able to function or are dead. You must learn the important elements of your departments quickly and run your organizations with extreme competence. I expect you all to be hands-on managers. Yes, you have to delegate much of what you are responsible for, but you must be aware of what is being done in your name. If the ax has to fall in a department, it is going to fall on your heads.

"Sara, as the first female Secretary of Defense, you are especially going to be under the microscope. Even though you wore three stars on an Army uniform, there will be those who will not look beyond the fact that you're a woman. You'll have to deal with that yourself in most situations. Some people might expect me to run in and protect you each time you're questioned about a decision you've made or a policy you've implemented, and I know you wouldn't want or need that. I have every confidence in each of you that you can handle the positions that you have, or you would not have been chosen. Be ready to take over in just under three weeks. Questions?"

"Have our security clearances come back yet from the FBI?" asked Fernando Gutierrez, the soon-to-be Secretary of State.

"Yes, you're all in possession of top security clearances. The only ones higher are those held by the Vice-President and myself. You will receive official notification from the FBI in the coming days, along with credentials specific to your area. Any other questions?" When no one spoke up, I continued, "In that case, this meeting is adjourned until this time next week. At that time, please have a list of names for your top deputies that need clearances. Remember, the transition team must sign off on all those chosen by you. We don't have a lot of time left, so please make sure you have the names or you run the risk of having vacant slots in your offices."

CHAPTER 4
MAKING HISTORY

It was January 19th, the day before the Inauguration. Special Agent Shane Thompson had returned from specialized training and was now by my side day and night. Everything was ready for the big day, and my stomach was in knots. The outgoing President had invited me to the White House on the 15th, just five days before I was to be sworn in. I informed him that my schedule would not permit me the time to call upon him at this late date, and that according to tradition, I would meet him at the White House on the 20th at 11:00 A.M. in order to ride to the Capitol together in the Presidential limousine.

The only really annoying thing was that the members of the diplomatic Corps from Muslim countries refused to attend my swearing in because of their views on homosexuality. They didn't realize they were setting the tone for relations between their countries and the United States for as long as I was President. They would pay the greater price for their ignorance. The only exception to this 'boycott' was the Kingdom of Saudi Arabia, for whom we were the biggest customer for oil as well as their arms supplier. Some things did trump religious principles, even for an Arab nation.

I had a 3:00 P.M. meeting with the Director of the Secret Service regarding the next day, and other issues relating to the protection of the others and myself who were their responsibility. During the meeting I was briefed on threat levels being monitored by the Secret Service. It seemed some people were determined that I would not be sworn in as President because I was gay. The Director wanted me to be always behind bullet resistant glass, and to not walk any part of the route from the Capitol to the White House. He also wanted me to wear a bullet resistant vest under my clothes for the entire inaugural day. Even though I had promised to cooperate with the

Service whenever I could, I balked at wearing a bullet resistant vest. The weather was extremely cold and therefore afforded me a perfectly good reason to stay in the limo instead of walking down Pennsylvania Avenue. The Director also asked for authority to hire and train more agents for the protection division since my presidency presented some unique challenges. I approved his request for thirty more agents, and I forwarded my authorization to the budget office for funding. His final request was flatly refused: I would not move the swearing in ceremony indoors and away from the people. My presidency would not be spent hiding from the violent elements of society. The people had the right to see their President take the Oath of Office that was mandatory every four years whether you were a new President or re- elected to a second term. The Director left the meeting feeling he had won some and lost some.

I then asked Agent Thompson to come into my office. It sure was good to see him again after he had been gone for a month and a half.

"Hello, Shane, how are you?"

"Fine, sir, good to be back."

"Are you ready for tomorrow?"

"Yes, sir, the entire Secret Service is on duty tomorrow to make sure you get where you need to go, in complete safety. Are there any special instructions for me, sir?"

"Well, which part of the day will you be with me?"

"Why, the entire day, sir. I'll meet you when you get up in the morning, and will leave you when you go to bed in the White House."

"That's going to be at least twenty hours," I protested. "You can't possibly be on duty that long!"

"Sir, I choose to remain with you. I'm your personal bodyguard from the Service, and I take my job seriously. I don't intend to let anything happen to you while you're in my care. I'll have all the required clothes, including a tuxedo for the Balls."

"Tell me something, Shane," I asked curiously. "What would be your reaction and that of the other agents if I should date someone while President?"

"I can only speak for myself, sir, but I would imagine the others are professionals and will do the job they're trained to do. Whether or not you are gay, you are still the President. As for me – well, sir, can I be frank?"

Fearing the worst, I steeled myself and said, "Of course, I wouldn't have it any other way. I take it my being gay makes you nervous?"

"Sir, please keep this between us, but I'm gay, too. Nothing about your sexuality makes me nervous."

Despite my earlier speculation, the confirmation I'd just received stunned me. Shane was gay? How could I possibly be so lucky as to have an agent who himself was gay?

"You're joking with me, right? Or are you just saying this to make me more comfortable with you seeing something that might upset other agents?"

"No, sir, I really am gay. The Service doesn't know it, of course, as they're very homophobic and I would have never been assigned to you as a candidate for President, let alone as President, if they did. I only admitted to myself that I was gay three years ago, so no one in the Secret Service knows anything. They assume I'm straight. Is that all right with you?"

"Is what all right with me, the fact that you're gay, or that the Secret Service doesn't know?"

"Well, sir, I guess both."

"For the first time, I feel like I can actually relax around someone from your organization. This has been an issue that's troubled me since I won the election. What privacy and ability to be myself would I really have with such close protection – that was the question. Now, I find out that my closest agent outside of the SAC of the Presidential Detail is also gay? I can't tell you how relieved I am,

Shane. Now I really welcome having you with me as much as your schedule allows."

"Great, sir, I feel much better now that you know, too. I want you to be comfortable with me and to know that I'll always have your best security interests at heart. You after all trust me with your life, not to mention the fact that since you chose me to be your personal bodyguard, you've advanced my career by a couple of decades."

I got up and made sure that no one was looking, before asking, "Can I give you a hug?"

"Of course, sir," he answered after also making sure that no one was watching.

I only held Shane in my arms briefly, but in those couple of moments, I felt the power and strength of his body. I was right, he was extremely well built, solid, and would be a formidable opponent to anyone trying to rush me.

I resisted the strong urge to kiss him on the temple, and released him after patting his back. He looked at me and smiled, his light green eyes sparkling.

"Thank you for that. You're the first man I've hugged in a while now who knows that I'm gay, and who is gay himself. I will respect our boundaries of course, but it felt nice to hold you however briefly."

"You're more than welcome, sir. And believe me when I say that it was my pleasure to hold you, something I would never have asked you to do. You're a very good looking man, and now the most powerful man in the world."

I smiled and looked down toward the floor only to have my eyes catch sight of a healthy bulge in Shane's pants. I quickly broke off my gaze and looked back up to see Shane turn pink from embarrassment.

"I'm sorry, sir, I'll make sure that never happens again," he said while quickly adjusting himself. "I'd better get back to my post now, unless there's something else?"

If Shane could only hear what I was thinking, he would know what else he could do for me.

"Don't apologize for a natural reaction. Just make sure it doesn't happen when others are around," I said with a laugh, which only served to unintentionally embarrass Shane further.

"Yes, sir, now I must really return to my post."

"We'll talk again in private, Shane. Thank you for sharing such precious information about yourself with me."

As Shane left the room, I once again tried to check out what I was now sure was a rock hard ass. But once again, his suit jacket covered the view I now wanted to see most urgently. I reveled in the knowledge that my personal bodyguard was gay, giving me a little more freedom than I would have had otherwise. I simply found it very hard to believe that out of the entire Secret Service, I drew perhaps the only agent who was not only gay, but young, good looking, and with great sexual appeal. I smiled remembering the bulge in Shane's pants, proof that he really was gay.

I reprimanded myself for all sorts of fantasies that broke out in my now fevered mind. How precious it would be to make love to him – it had been a long time since I made love to such a man. It was going to be difficult now to look at Shane in the same way as I did before I knew he was gay.

It was just past six in the evening and the tension and anticipation of the events of the next day had only grown stronger. When my staff asked me where I wanted to have dinner, I informed them that I wasn't hungry and would have a light snack later in the evening. I intended to go to bed by 11:00 P.M. so I didn't have much time left to tie up any loose ends. As I went over my schedule with Mary for Inauguration Day, I realized that every minute from the time I got up until bedtime was accounted for with either a function or a duty. I would need my sleep tonight. I released Shane just after seven o'clock and told him to get plenty of rest as tomorrow was going to be a fun but difficult day.

I spent the next two hours receiving phone calls from world leaders and others offering their congratulations on my impending oath of office. These would be crucial contacts for the successful conduct of foreign policy and crisis intervention during my Administration. America needed all the friends she could get and to mend all of the fences broken over the last decade by an uncaring, arrogant power hungry theocrat. I had a lot of work to do to repair the image and prestige of the United States and I was determined to succeed.

At ten minutes past eleven, I said good night to my staff and went to sleep at Blair House where we had relocated that morning. Blair House was the official guesthouse of the United States Government and was used to house visiting heads of state as well as, upon occasion, the sitting United States President. Harry Truman and his family were forced to stay at Blair House when the White House underwent extensive renovations due to the rotting wood found in the floors and support beams of the White House. It was an elegant house inside, but small in size. It would be a short trip in the morning to finalize the transfer of power, as Blair was located across from the White House itself.

Considering all that was about to happen, I was surprisingly well rested when I was woken at 6:00 A.M. by my valet. I sprang out of bed, quickly showered and dressed in casual clothes to eat before putting on the more formal dress used for the oath of office. I opened the door and true to his word, Shane was already on duty and standing outside.

"Good morning, sir, I hope you slept well."

"Good morning, Shane, and yes, surprisingly, I slept very well. Time for breakfast."

Shane followed me, speaking into his hand microphone as we went, "Condor One is on the move to the second floor dining room."

There was a new phrase that I would soon get very used to hearing. "Condor One" was my Secret Service code name and indicated to those in the know that the President was doing something. At this point all the President-elect wanted to do was drink coffee and orange juice. As I entered the dining room, everyone either stood up if they were sitting, or froze in place.

"Good morning, everyone, I hope you're all ready for the big day, because it's here!"

A resounding chorus of good morning was returned to me, and everyone simply clapped.

"Okay, you're going spoil me and I'm going want you all to clap every morning when I come to breakfast, so you'd better knock that off," I said with a smile.

As I sat down, the morning Washington Post and New York Times were handed to me. My coffee was poured and I quickly scanned the headlines. All of them dealt with the pending Inaugural Day and speculation on who would be with me when I made an appearance at the twenty-two Inaugural Balls that were slated for this evening. I had to smile, finding it slightly amusing that the press was so preoccupied with my dating and love life. What would they do if I actually showed up at the Balls with some twinkie or better yet, a male Hollywood celebrity? I laughed aloud.

"Something funny on the front page of the Post? I find that hard to believe," Mary observed.

"No, just amusing myself with what the press finds interesting regarding my single status."

"Ah, let them guess and worry about it, they have nothing better to do anyway."

Mary was sixty-four years old with auburn hair, brown eyes, widowed already, with three grown children and six grandchildren. She was sharp, smart, and loyal and held a Masters Degree in communication. She was all that I could ask for in someone so important to the everyday life of a President.

The man who I chose to be my Chief of Staff was forty-two year old Andrew J. Carter, a man who had roamed the corridors of Washington for the last sixteen years and who had been my first choice to take this vital position on my personal team. Carter was the former

Chief of Staff to the House Minority leader and someone I had met years ago in business. Everyone applauded my choosing him because as an insider, he knew how to get things done in a heavily bureaucratic town. Many people knew Carter so they felt they would have an easier task getting to me through someone that they knew.

After finishing my coffee and the scan of the newspapers, I received more phone calls from well-wishers who knew me from the business world. I also intended to keep my business contacts alive and well, knowing I would have to call upon the captains of industry to help get the economy back on track. The economy was another present the outgoing Administration was leaving me. When they took over, they were handed a surplus in the Treasury and now were leaving with the nation trillions of dollars in debt and a recession that was just settling in.

They made sure that I had as many problems as possible starting out.

At precisely 10:55, the official Presidential limousine pulled up in front of Blair House and I took my seat for the very short ride across the street to meet with the outgoing President. The man who would from now on be my driver, Special Agent Edward K. Spence was behind the wheel, with the detail leader in the right front seat. Since I had no wife, I was the only one in the rear compartment. Shane was walking alongside the car by my door as we drove across the street. Arriving at the North Portico, I saw President Scalia waiting out front for me, as was the normal procedure. Shane opened my car door and I got out and shook the hand Scalia offered. There was no smile on his face, no warmth in his voice as he greeted me.

"Good morning Mr. Windsor. I trust you're ready to assume the duties of the President?"

"Indeed I am or I wouldn't be standing here. Shall we go in?"

"By all means, you know the way – oh, I guess you don't. This is your first visit to the White House, isn't it?"

"Yes it is, too bad that your schedule didn't allow for the normal process to unfold. But never fear, I have competent staff and we were able to do or get everything I needed. It will be a refreshing change for this old house, won't it?"

Before he realized what I had said, he replied, "Yes, it will be."

I merely smiled at the man who had wrecked the country while President. I could tell he was still thinking about what I had said, trying to figure out if he had been insulted or not, when we arrived at a small receiving room off the entranceway where coffee was waiting for us, once again, as tradition dictated. This was the time when the outgoing President normally informed the incoming President of anything of a high security nature that he didn't already know. If there were a Stargate in existence, for example, now would be the time for him to tell me. But instead of state secrets, Scalia only told me that he had left a letter for me on the desk in the Oval Office for when I returned from the swearing-in ceremony. A butler served the coffee, which I ignored and which Scalia drank. He was barely able to make small talk with me until we were scheduled to get into the limo for the ride to the Capitol. It was obvious that I was Scalia's worst nightmare: a gay man with the military behind him.

At 11:45, an aide to Scalia informed him that it was time for him to leave the White House for the last time and head to the Capitol. Hiding a smile at Scalia's sigh of relief, I rose and followed him to the portico where everyone was waiting for us. The sitting President got into the limo first followed by the soon-to-be President. As I was getting into the limo, I looked up and saw a quick smile flash across Shane's face. I couldn't resist the chance to give him a dig and said, "Enjoy your jog," as I smiled back to him. Shane would have to jog along side of the limo as we went up to the Capitol at a slow speed, which allowed the agents to keep up with Limo One.

Scalia failed to smile even one time all the way to the Capitol. He spoke not one word and the air was like a sheet of ice. This man really couldn't stand the fact that I was going to be President in a few short minutes. As we arrived at the Capitol and awaited the signal to alight from the limo, I said to Scalia, "By the way, just to let you know, when I return to the White House shortly, I am issuing ten Executive Orders reversing ten Orders that you issued as President. If you're curious as to which ones, just read the morning papers."

Scalia grew red in the face but before he could explode, the car door was yanked open and Shane stuck his head into the compartment. Ignoring Scalia, he said directly to me, "All's clear, sir."

Scalia practically jumped out of the limo and began mumbling to himself. Neither I nor anyone near me could make out what he said. It was customary for us to walk side by side all the way to our seats on the Capitol platform for the ceremony; however, Scalia just shot ahead of me and arrived first on the platform, leaving me without the proper escort, not that I could blame him. I merely smiled when asked by the Master at Arms of the House of Representatives if everything was all right. I continued to shake hands that were offered to me as I made my way through the crowd with Shane close by my side watching every hand, every movement of those in our path.

Suddenly as we moved through the statuary hall, a hand with a gun stuck out from the crowd directly in front and two feet ahead of me. As the arm began to pivot, aiming directly at me, Shane shouted, "GUN!" and shoved me to the floor, covering me with his body.

At the shout of "Gun," the other agents on my detail sprang into action. Weapons were drawn including Uzis pulled from specially built briefcases, which allowed an agent to produce an automatic weapon in less than two seconds. Just as the agents began to rush the gunman, a shot rang out from the man's weapon, missing Shane, hitting the marble floor and ricocheting off to strike Senator William Mitchell, an ultra-conservative Republican Senator from Mississippi. The two agents nearest to the gunman both opened fire, striking the suspect and killing him instantly.

Total and complete pandemonium broke out throughout the hall as people screamed and ran, trampling others who had fallen down, or not gotten up from diving to the floor when the gunshot rang out. Twenty or more firearms were now in evidence as every police officer and Secret Service Agent had pulled their weapon.

Suddenly I heard Shane whisper into my ear, "Get up, stay with me, and don't stop for anything." I was pulled to my feet by three agents and propelled into a holding room off the main hallway that led into the hall of statues. The room was small but totally contained with multiple layers of security now in place to prevent any further access to me.

"Sir, you must remain here until we secure the area, determine who the gunman was, and if there are any other security breaches."

"The gunman is dead?"

"Yes, sir, shot and killed by other agents on your detail. He was dead before he hit the floor. Bad thing is, we won't be able to question him. For the next few minutes, we aren't letting anyone in here. We call this a protective cocoon. Are you injured, sir? Do you need a medic?"

"No, but I am a little bruised; I think from hitting the floor so hard."

"Well, sir, that's a lot better than being dead right now."

"Okay, do what you have to do, but be careful, Shane, and thank you for saving my life. I won't forget it."

"It's my job, sir, but in this case, I'm even happier that I was by your side."

Before I could reply, he left the room. Scalia was informed on the platform what had happened and the first question he asked was, "Is he dead?"

"Yes, sir, the Secret Service killed the gunman."

"No, not the gunman, Windsor, is Windsor dead?"

"No, sir, the President-elect is perfectly safe and will be secured until the area is once again cleared."

Scalia sat down with a sour look on his face. He leaned over to his Vice-President and whispered something to him. An official with the Inaugural committee walked up to the microphone and notified the crowd that there was to be a short delay before the ceremony began. The crowd began to murmur as the current President was already on the dais, and therefore the new President was the delay. The press immediately smelled a story and shortly became aware that someone had tried to kill the incoming President. As word spread through the crowd of what had actually happened, people started to surge toward the dais and police were forced to use limited force to keep them out of the security zone. Sketchy details of the attempted assassination were flashed around the world.

Five minutes passed before Shane re-entered the holding room and announced that the area had been cleared, and I would be able to securely get to the dais if I insisted on taking the Oath of Office in public.

"Yes, we will proceed according to plan. Let's get moving, we are almost ten minutes behind schedule, and Scalia has been President longer than is tolerable."

I left the room and was swiftly moved the short distance to the dais surrounded by a phalanx of bodyguards. Everyone stood and applauded my safe arrival. Even Scalia was on his feet, although he wasn't clapping.

At 12:15, my number two took the Oath of Office as Vice-President. At 12:18, the Chief Justice of the Supreme Court of the United States administered the short but concise Oath of Office to me.

"I, David James Windsor, do solemnly swear that I will faithfully execute the office of President of the United States, and will to the best of my ability, preserve, protect and defend the Constitution of the United States."

The Chief Justice shook my hand, and with that, I was the President. Scalia was now the former President with no power whatsoever over the United States Government. It was a good day for America. The crowd cheered, and 'Hail to the Chief' was played for me for the first time while the Army Old Guard fired a twenty-one-gun salute. History had been made, both for America, the world, and for the gay community. It was time for my Inaugural speech. As I looked out over the assembled witnesses and the crisp blue winter sky, I was filled with a sense of destiny. It was within my power to help to create a better world, a world where war might be less prevalent, and mankind might damage the environment less. I began to settle down somewhat from both the danger of the attempted assassination, and the high of being sworn in as President. Once again, my gaze fell upon the people in the seats below and beyond.

"My fellow Americans, it is a grand day in America when a new Administration comes into power in Washington filled with the expectation of achievement, with the desire to do what is right for the citizens of this country. But what is right for the people?

"The people have the right to be secure in their possessions, secure in their freedom from unreasonable search and seizure, secure in their right to pursue happiness and the American dream. They also have the right to health care, security in old age, the expectation of privacy and national security in situations that call for such security. Finally, the most important right that the American people possess is the right to the knowledge that their government will act in accordance with their best interests and not only the interests of those who are wealthy or in positions of power and influence. My Administration will always serve the will of the people and perform the functions that government is meant to serve. We will fight those who wish to destroy the freedoms that this democracy offers to the citizens of this country, and will resist without ceasing any attempt to diminish these same freedoms that our forefathers fought for and won for this great nation.

"But as President, I intend to make the lives of the people better than they have been, not just to maintain the status quo. We will be creative in approaches to old problems such as pollution, disease, and hunger. We will fight the epidemic of homeless veterans of the wars of the past administration so that our men and women of the Armed Forces know that they mean more to America than just being disposable soldiers on the battlefield. Veterans have the right to know that we will do everything we can for them after they return from the front. We will endeavor to provide outstanding health care, both physical and mental, for problems that arose from their service to this country. Returning veterans have the right to a job to insure a smooth transition from military service to civilian life instead of ending up in homeless shelters and on the street. Walter Reed and Bethesda Naval hospitals will once again be symbols of pride in our care of our wounded personnel, insuring that the latest in technology and medicine is used to put our people back on the road to recovery.

"I promise the American people and the members of the Armed Forces that I will never use you lightly. If I send you to war, know that the United States had no other choice. To our potential enemies, know that this Administration will provide the absolute best in equipment, technology and leadership to our military so that we are second to none.

"To the internal enemies of democracy that tried only a few minutes ago to subvert the will of the people, know this: I will use every asset available to me and this Administration to defeat your efforts to destabilize the political process and change the will of the people. You will fail. I warn you, do not be mistaken in your beliefs about who I am, and what I am capable of – I do not scare easily. I urge you to work with us to build a better America instead of trying to tear down the pillars of democracy. A full investigation of the attempted assault upon my person that took place within the walls of the Capitol a short while ago will be undertaken and the people behind this outrageous attempt to alter the will of the people will be identified, arrested, tried and convicted. Make no mistake about it; I am determined to bring the government of the people back to the people, so help me God."

As applause broke out across the lawn of the Capitol and in the seats behind me, I waved to the people, not realizing that Scalia and his immediate entourage had left their seats and were walking off the dais. Only when I turned around to shake the hand of Vice-President Miller did I realize what had happened.

HALFWAY across the nation, a man threw a glass of Scotch through the television screen he was watching, and asked rhetorically, "Can you fucking believe this?"

THE head of the Presidential protection detail walked up and waited for me to break away from Miller.

"Mr. President, in light of what happened forty minutes ago, I urge you to cancel your appearance at the Capitol luncheon and head directly to the Presidential limousine where you can be encased in protection."

"Have you been able to determine anything yet about the gunman?"

"No, sir, he carried no identification, nothing, even his clothing had no labels. The FBI has already taken fingerprints off the body and is running them through NCIC to try to get a match. If that fails, we may not know who the man was for some time."

"Agent McDowell, I can't run and hide every time there is a threat or I would be paralyzed trying to run this government. Please secure the route to the luncheon, and double check all wait staff. Put some men in the food service area, and when the lunch is over, secure the route to the car. Run the bomb dogs through everywhere and that should do it, don't you think?"

"Mr. President, if that is your wish, then we will do our best to protect you. But I intend to allow no one in the hallways while you are in motion, and would request that you at least cut the lunch short."

"Very well, I think that is reasonable. Give me the signal when it's secure for me to move from here. After all, we are behind a wall of bullet resistant glass."

"Yes sir, everyone is being held here until you are off of the dais. It should be just a few moments."

As I sat down in the chair for the President, aides rushed up to me asking if I was all right. I assured everyone that the Secret Service had done their job and that I had obviously survived the attack. Shane practically stood on top of me, which gave me the first chance to speak with him since the incident.

"Agent Thompson, I want to thank you for your quick action this morning, you probably saved my life. The fact that you actually did throw yourself on me, putting yourself in the path of any bullets, is beyond commendable, it's extraordinary. I obviously made the right choice for my close-in agent."

"Mr. President, they always told us that if something were to happen, it would be over in mere seconds and that our instant unhesitant reaction could be the difference between life and death for the protectee. I'm grateful you're unharmed, sir."

"Thank you again, and I'm also pleased that you're unharmed. What happened to the Senator that was hit?"

"Sorry to inform you, sir, but Senator Mitchell was killed instantly from a gunshot to the head. The round fired at you missed, ricocheted off the floor and struck the Senator. He never had a chance," Shane told me.

"Andy, make sure you coordinate with the Senator's family and if they want a state funeral for the Senator, we'll give him one. Let me know when you know."

"Yes, Mr. President."

"Sir, I've been advised that it is clear to move you to the lunch room, shall we go?"

"Yes, let's get this over with."

Exiting from the dais, I was surrounded once again by a heavy Secret Service presence and we moved through empty corridors, led by agents with German Shepherds that were trained in the detection of bombs as well as hidden humans. When we reached the location of the luncheon, it was immediately sealed after I entered the room. In total, there were twelve agents with me including of course Shane Thompson, and Andy, my Chief of Staff. As soon as I entered the room, the Speaker of the House, my former opponent, came up to me and expressed great dismay at the attempt on my life. I honestly couldn't tell if he was sincere or not.

"Mr. President, I am so glad that you are all right! This is terrible, that on your Inaugural Day, someone tried to assassinate you."

"Thank you, Mr. Speaker. What the Secret Service and I want to know is how the man penetrated Capitol security on Inauguration Day and almost assassinated the incoming President. This reflects badly on the Capitol Police as well as the Congressional Sergeant at Arms."

"Yes, Mr. President, I agree with you. I can assure you of the full cooperation of the Congress in this matter. A full investigation will take place and those responsible for the failure of security will be brought to task for this incident."

"Let's skip the speeches today, have lunch and allow for my quick departure. The Secret Service wanted me to cancel this engagement altogether, and this is the compromise that I agreed to."

"While I'm disappointed that the speeches won't be made, I understand completely. Let me introduce you to the guests."

"Ladies and gentlemen, due to the shocking events of an hour ago, the President is cutting short his visit with us and we will do without the usual speeches. Therefore, it is my privilege to introduce to you the new President of the United States, David Windsor."

"Thank you, Mr. Speaker. Again, I apologize for curtailing the speeches, but I have agreed to cooperate with the Secret Service as much as possible during my Presidency. So, without further delay, let us enjoy lunch."

The meal was quickly served under the very watchful eyes of the Secret Service, which included the Director himself who had responded to the Capitol when he was notified of the shooting. The area was sealed so tight, not even a cockroach could have crawled into the room unnoticed. As lunch finished up, the Director asked if he could speak with me privately. I motioned for Shane to remain where he was as I walked with the Director to an empty corner of the room.

"Mr. President, I must ask if you will consider a strong curtailment of public appearances until we figure out who the assassin was and if others are involved. We haven't lost a President since JFK even though Reagan was shot, and I don't intend to lose a President while I'm Director."

"I'll make that call on a case by case basis, Director. I will not live in constant fear of being harmed and lock myself away in the White House. Too many people would rejoice at that spectacle. By the way, I'm requesting that the Secret Service award Agent Thompson a Medal for Valor for his actions this morning. He put his life in direct danger by throwing himself on me and could have easily been killed instead of me. I know that's what they train for, but actually doing it is another matter. If that had happened in the military, he would qualify for nomination for the Congressional Medal of Honor."

"Of course, Mr. President. I will see to it that he gets the Service's Medal of Valor for his actions in the line of duty."

"Also, I want his assignment to me made permanent. It gives me great comfort to have him around, especially after this morning."

"Consider it done, Mr. President. He will not be reassigned without your okay."

"Excellent, thank you, Director. Okay, I'm ready to head to the White House. Will you get things underway?"

"Yes, sir."

The Director spoke into his hand mic and agents of the Secret Service seemed to move in unison. Shane and two other agents escorted me to the Speaker to say my goodbyes, while others prepared to open the door and move to the motorcade.

"Thank you, Mr. Speaker, for your hospitality. I must go now, but I want to assure you that the luncheon was great in spite of today's events. I look forward to working with you as the Speaker."

"Thank you, Mr. President, for not canceling the luncheon altogether. I personally appreciate your efforts to keep tradition alive. Enjoy the rest of your day, and I will see you tonight at the Mayflower Hotel Ball."

"Until then, Mr. Speaker."

Turning toward the door lit a fire under the rest of my detail and once again agents surrounded me. The dogs led the way again as we moved quickly to the side Portico and the waiting motorcade. As I got into the Presidential limo, I turned to Shane and requested that he ride inside with me. He spoke into his mic, and another agent immediately took his place at the right rear of the limo as Shane got inside and sat across from me in the seat that faced backwards. He was also out of view for the most part in that position.

As we began to move, Shane smiled at me, and I returned the smile. Before I could stop myself, my eyes wandered down to his crotch, which appeared full and inviting. Shane saw me looking at his goods, and smiled even broader and spread his legs just a little further apart. It was now my turn to sprout wood with a smile. When Shane noticed the physiological change in my pants, he smiled and said, "Now, we're even."

I broke out laughing for the first time that day as I adjusted myself. Shane watched and continued to smile. His smile left his face as we turned onto Pennsylvania Avenue and all of his attention went to the crowds that lined the street. In turn, I directed my attention to the crowd and waved at the people as we went by at a faster pace than was usual for this part of the inaugural day. The streets were heavily lined, with many gay and lesbian people attending as evidenced by the various rainbow colored objects. I felt a certain level of pride that they were acknowledging this day as one as much for them as it was for me.

Before I knew it, we had arrived at the White House, traveling through the main gate and up to the ceremonial entrance. Since Shane was inside the limo, another agent opened the door, and I got out first with Shane following me. The chief domestic employee of the White House, the head usher, greeted me just outside the door.

"Good afternoon, Mr. President, welcome home."

"Hello, thank you, it's good to be here in the people's house."

"This way, sir," the doorman said as he bowed slightly and showed me inside with a wave of his hand.

As I entered the White House, I was asked if I would like to go to the residence to change and relax for a few minutes. My reply was yes, I would. I was shown to an elevator that was reserved for only the President and got into it along with no one but Shane and the head butler. We got off at the second floor residence, and I was shown around by the head butler who escorted me through the President's bedroom, the Lincoln bedroom, the Rose bedroom, as well as two smaller bedrooms, and common areas like the family dining room, living room, library and a small bar.

I noticed that my own private furniture and things had been brought in and placed around while I was at the Capitol. I was right; the entire residence was tacky and would need some work to bring it up to par. I realized that without a wife and any children, I would be the sole occupant of the private residence. That felt slightly lonely. An idea started to take form. I didn't know if it would work, but I would try.

"Henry, would you wait in the family room while I speak with Agent Thompson here?"

"Of course, Mr. President. Would you like anything to drink while you are here?"

"Yes, a diet 7-up will be my usual non-alcoholic drink."

"Of course, sir, it will be waiting for you when you come out."

As he walked away, I motioned for Shane to join me in the dining room.

"Shane, I'm going to be all alone up here with no family to move into this place. Would you consider taking a room here, and living in the residence?"

A look of complete shock crossed Shane's face.

"Are you serious, Mr. President? No Secret Service Agent has ever lived in the White House."

"Look, JFK not only had a friend who practically lived here in his own room, he was in fact gay, a fact that seemed to disturb everyone but the President. I was almost assassinated before I could even take the Oath of Office, so it won't seem strange that I asked for my personal agent to be close around the clock. It's an easy thing to explain and then it will be forgotten. Plus when you're officially off duty, you can have the benefits of living at the White House."

"What might those benefits be?" he asked with a smile.

I immediately knew what he meant, smiled, and smacked Shane on the arm.

"Bad boy, now stop that, or you'll be giving me ideas."

"Well, off duty, that's what I was wondering about," he replied without a smile. "I've gotten to know you fairly well over the last fourteen months, and I not only respect you, I admire you as well as like you. Now, nothing more has to occur than that, unless you decide otherwise. I can remain your close-in agent, totally professional at all times, or I can remain your close-in agent, totally professional while on duty. Whatever you decide, sir, you have my complete agreement. Were I to live here at the White House, it would make other things possible and much easier for both of us. Please forgive me if I've spoken out of turn."

"No, nothing to forgive, Shane. I've grown very fond of you, too, and that was before this morning. To be honest, I've desired something far more personal from you, but never dreamed that it was possible. Let's say this: you agree to live here at the residence, and we'll see what develops from there, nothing forced, agree?"

"Yes, Mr. President, that sounds very sensible."

"Very well, then that's settled. I will inform the domestic staff, and you take care of notification to the Secret Service. If you start to hear jokes about you living here, let me know and I'll quash them."

"That won't be necessary, sir; I can handle any jokes and take care of them myself."

As we walked to the living room, the butler met us, carrying a tray with not one, but two sodas on it. "I brought a soda for your agent also, sir, in case he was thirsty as well."

"Excellent, Henry, that was thoughtful of you. Would you inform whoever it concerns that Agent Thompson here will be moving into the residence and living here while I am President? I would like him to have the best room feasible here in the immediate residence versus the other wing."

"Yes, Mr. President, that would be the office of the usher and I will take care of that now, if you're not in need of anything else at the moment. When will the Agent be moving in?"

I turned to look at Shane, raising my eyebrows in question.

"I can begin to live here tomorrow, Henry. Is that too soon?

"No, Agent Thompson, nothing of that sort is too fast around here. We simply get the number of people required to accomplish something, and then make it happen."

"Outstanding, Henry, thank you for taking care of this important matter for me."

"That's why I'm here, sir, to take care of anything that you require. If you'll excuse me, Mr. President, I'll attend to this now."

Shane and I walked over and sat down in the President's private living room and sipped our 7-up's. Before we could talk any further, the phone rang next to the sofa, and I picked it up.

"President Windsor."

"Sir, this is Andy. You're due at the reviewing stand in ten minutes."

"Okay, Andy, I'll be down in four minutes."

"We have to go shortly; I'm supposed to be on the reviewing stand."

"Very well, I've heard nothing on my ear piece that indicates any problems at this time."

"Before we go, Shane, I want to emphasize two things. One, you do not have to live here at the White House if you don't wish to, and two, if you do live here, you do not have to do anything other than your duties with the Secret Service, you realize this, right?"

"Sir, do you think for one moment I would have even entertained such an idea under Scalia? I would have rather lived with a pack of rats than live under the same roof as that clown."

"Okay, Shane, just making sure. I love that you'll be just down the hall from me."

"Or maybe lying right next to you."

At that statement, I got up and walked over to Shane. "Stand up."

"Sir, I didn't mean to offend you by saying that," he replied while standing.

Before he could say another word, I kissed him directly on the lips and felt no resistance. I put my arms around him as he did me. We kissed for another few seconds and then broke it off before anyone walked in and caught us.

"Thank you, Shane, for that pleasure. Now shall we go downstairs and permit me to once again act as President instead of horny teenage boy?"

"I don't know which role I prefer more, sir," he said with a broad smile.

We got into the elevator marked President and arrived at the first floor. There was a group of aides and agents waiting for us, Shane having informed the people on the mic network that I was moving towards the ground floor. I soon learned that it was nearly impossible for me to move anywhere without at least a dozen people and a command post knowing where I was and where I was headed. It really would have been almost impossible to have any kind of secret love life such as JFK had when he was President. He was able to sneak away and have affairs on a fairly regular basis but in his time, the press and the various government agencies concerned with the President were discreet and didn't tell. Was that what made Shane so appealing to me? Was it that we could have a love life fairly easily without being caught? I honestly could answer 'no' to that question. I was attracted to Shane the moment he had joined my detail when I was just a candidate. No, this went far deeper than mere convenience; it went all the way to the heart.

We all walked down the White House driveway where I took my place in the reviewing stands to witness the Inaugural parade. First came the troops for which I stood to acknowledge their respect paid to me as Commander in Chief. This filled me with pride for our nation as I witnessed the young men and women of the Armed Services march past their President. There were no tanks or other battle armaments as that was not the custom for our country as it was in Russia or China. The only thing that mattered was the people who served their country. The parade ended about ninety minutes after it had started with various high school bands that had been chosen to march in the parade as an honor for their school and home state.

CHAPTER 5
THE FIRST NIGHT

As we reentered the White House, I was met by the head usher who informed me that all arrangements to accommodate Shane were underway.

"Mr. President, in accordance with your wishes, your Agent will be one door down from you in the residence. Is that all right sir?"

"Yes, Mr. Frank, that works out well, thank you."

"Of course, sir. If you require anything else, just phone my office and I will see to it personally."

"Very good."

"Where to now, sir?" asked Shane.

"To the Oval Office to read a letter left by the former occupant."

Shane spoke into his mic, "Condor One in route to the Oval Office."

Walking into the Oval office for the first time as President gave me a very strange but heavy feeling. This was where the potential fate of the world could be decided on a number of issues. The office was well cleaned and tidy, with a letter sitting in the middle of the desk which bore no other item than the phone. Mary came in behind me and said, "Welcome to your world, Mr. President."

"Indeed, Mary. Would you have this desk changed out for the Kennedy desk? This one looks as if it were made in a steel yard somewhere."

"Yes, sir, I'll make the call now."

I sat down behind the desk and opened the envelope marked with the simple notation, "For the President."

"Dear President Windsor: I leave this office in your hands not completely happy with the fact that a gay is replacing me. I believe it would have been far better to have Mr. Gorski taking over this office than you. However, you are the President and as such you will have my full support as it relates to our national security. Please feel free to call upon me in any situation where my experience might better enable you to make the correct decision as it affects said security.

"Good luck, Mr. Windsor, you're going to need a lot of it."

The letter was signed simply, "Scalia."

"Ha, here's a letter for posterity. Scalia doesn't like the fact that a 'gay' replaced him, but he's more than willing to help said 'gay' out if the country is contemplating war. Well, fuck him."

"He just can't stand the fact that he's no longer in power, that's all."

"Well, Shane, like I said, fuck 'em. We have two hours until I have to be at the first Ball. I'd like to lie down for a half hour before eating and dressing. I'm going upstairs, why don't you take a break since we'll be going strong until around two A.M.?"

"Okay, I can relax in your living room while you sleep. I'm still on duty, sir."

"Actually, after tomorrow, it will be our living room," I said with a smile.

"Yes, sir, it will be."

I'd been asleep for thirty minutes when my valet woke me up and asked when I would be ready to eat. I sat up in bed, not recognizing for a moment where I was – was it all a dream?

"I'll eat in ten minutes, James; will you ask Agent Thompson if he would like to dine with me?"

"Of course, sir. Ten minutes."

I got out of bed and threw on some casual clothes that had been laid out for me next to the eveningwear for tonight. The Presidential bedroom was large but not huge. There was a king size bed, dressers, a sofa, two easy chairs, a fireplace, and a small worktable. There was, of course, an in-room bathroom that had the latest in showerheads. There were phones, phones everywhere you turned. It was evident that if they needed the President, they wanted a phone nearby.

When I came out of my bedroom, I found not only Shane, but another agent as well. I shot Shane a questioning glance, which drew only a slight nod of his head. As I entered the dining room, I saw that only one place was set, and I sat down. A waiter immediately served dinner that consisted of Dutch split pea soup, a salad, and a small steak and baked potato. It was more than adequate and I tried to ignore the fact that I was eating alone. I ate quickly and waved off dessert and coffee. It was now 6:45, and it was time to dress for the evening. I returned to my bedroom and donned the formal dress for the evening celebration Balls.

When I came out of the bedroom, I found both agents dressed in tuxedos, Shane looking like he had just stepped out of a magazine. He really was a beautiful man and the tuxedo served to further highlight his looks. As I headed towards the elevator, I heard Shane advise the network I was on the move.

When I stepped off the elevator I was once again met by a large contingent of Secret Service agents, aides, and household staff. It was 7:20, and I headed towards the Oval Office. As I arrived, I was informed by Mary that Buckingham Palace was on the phone for me. I sat down at the desk and picked up the phone.

"President Windsor here."

"Good evening, Mr. President, this is King William, how are you?"

"Fine, William, and how are you?"

"I'm good, cousin; I just wanted to call you on your first evening as President and congratulate you on your incredible achievement, and to wish you well. I know you'll be an outstanding President. America is lucky to have you."

"Thank you, William, but a good part of America doesn't agree with your last statement, I'm afraid. Nonetheless, I do appreciate your good wishes."

"Ah, I imagine you're referring to the gay thing. Well, America has much growing up to do in that area, and they haven't realized yet how lucky they are to have you."

"Well, England has a King, and America has a Queen," I said with a laugh.

It took a good ten seconds for the King of England to cease his laughter.

"Cousin, I love you. I'd say the Windsors are doing quite well in the twenty-first century, wouldn't you?"

"Indeed. I'll be gone in four to eight years though, while you will still be upon your throne for years to come, no doubt."

"If God wills it, yes. Look, I'm sure you're incredibly busy, so I'll let you go. I also wanted to invite you to visit with us upon your first overseas trip. Is that possible?"

"Of course. I'd be delighted to see you and the rest of the family. I'll be in touch when it looks like I can manage that."

"Good show. I'll be off now, enjoy your evening, David."

"Thank you, Your Majesty."

I smiled to myself as I hung up, still enjoying my own comment about kings and queens, when Mary knocked on the door and came into the office.

"Mr. President, it's time for you to leave and begin your round of appearances at all the Inaugural Balls. I don't imagine you'll be back before two or three tomorrow morning."

"No, I don't anticipate being back sooner than that either. Why don't you join me at one of the balls?"

"Sir, I have to have my office up and running for tomorrow, and I need to know how to make everything work so that I don't have to tell you I don't know."

I smiled at Mary and said, "How did I get so lucky in finding you?"

"You're just lucky, that's all," she said with a laugh.

Everyone would want to be friends with Mary as she was one of the few gatekeepers this close to the President. She could control whose phone calls were passed into me, and who got an appointment to see me. I trusted her totally and knew she would not abuse that power.

As I got into the limousine, I noticed that my motorcade consisted of twelve vehicles, most of which were Secret Service 'War Wagons'. These were SUVs that each held four to five Secret Service agents who were heavily armed. In some of the SUVs, the rear window was open, and a Secret Service agent sat looking out with an M-16 or shotgun between his legs. This enabled the Service to see in all directions for any potential threat. After the incident at the Capitol, the Service was extra nervous and cautious and it showed.

The vehicles that were not just for Secret Service were other limos, one a backup for Limo One, and the other limos held Administration VIPs and key staff. I travelled alone once again, with Shane attending to his normal duties and riding in the vehicle directly behind mine. When we arrived at the Mayflower Hotel, Shane was out of his vehicle and to my door in a matter of a few seconds. I waited until the area was secure, which did not take long as we had driven into the underground garage of the Mayflower, where an advance detail of agents and police were waiting for my arrival.

Shane opened my door, allowing me to exit the limo, and escorted me to an elevator that took us to the ballroom floor. I entered the ballroom through a secure side door, and the crowd broke into a mighty cheer, with applause following my entrance for two full minutes. My mother who would be my dance partner for the evening was brought in separately by another detail and joined me on the stage. I did not want her traveling with me due to the increased security threat. She would spend the night at the White House, but I did not want her with me prior to this moment. It was one less thing I had to be worried about.

I made the speech that would be repeated almost word for word for the rest of the night. This particular Ball honored the most valuable contributors of the campaign, as was tradition. They were the bankers, stockbrokers, lawyers, doctors, and other professionals who either contributed themselves or arranged for millions of dollars in donations to be made to the campaign. Without such people, no federal or state election would be possible until public financing of all elections was the norm.

After the speech was finished, the music started up and I joined my mother on stage for the first official dance of the night as well as of my Presidency. It was odd having everyone in the ballroom focused just on us as we danced around the stage. Finally, the crowd joined in, and I began to enjoy myself, all under the watchful eye of Shane.

After the dance had finished, a tray was brought out to me with a glass of champagne on it. The crowd became quiet and I gave a toast to all those present who had helped me gain the Presidency. Glasses were raised, champagne was sipped, and everyone smiled and clapped after they put down their glasses. I said my goodbyes to the assembled and quickly moved off the stage and into the security corridor. My mother exited the opposite way and was moved on to the next location, until it was time to appear at the GLBT Ball, which was the last Ball of the night. I was the first President to actually make an appearance at a Ball put on for and by the gay community. Bill Clinton had taped a special message that was played at the gay Balls held in his honor, but he did not actually appear at either one.

When we arrived at the Washington Hilton, the site of the GLBT Ball, I felt a sense of relaxation wash over me. These were my people even more so than every other American I had been with this evening. These people knew what it was like to be gay in America and my election proved to them that anything was possible, even if you are gay.

The entrance to the ballroom operated like a well-oiled machine once again. Only this time, the applause was positively deafening and went on for more than ten minutes. Finally when order was restored, I began my speech. This one was slightly different than at the other Balls, acknowledging the efforts put into my campaign by the gay community both before and after I was outed by the Speaker of the House. I was the first openly gay President, and for the first time in the lives of everyone present, they knew their President would do nothing that would harm them for as long as he was in the White House. Even with Clinton, disappointment soon set in with the 'Don't ask, don't tell' policy and other failures at bettering the lives of gay citizens.

After my speech and toast came time for the traditional first official dance of that particular Ball. Everyone wondered who I would dance with; would I dance with my mother or not dance at all? When the music started, it was not a slow dance but rather an old song from the all boy band, 'N Sync. What better partner to dance with to the song, 'Dirty Pop,' than Lance Bass? There was no formal introduction; he just walked out on stage from behind the curtain. Slowly, the crowd recognized who he was and applause began for Lance as well as for me as the crowd realized that their President, who was gay, was going to dance with a man. I had to admit, Lance's dancing ability had improved with age and I had a great time on stage with him. My eyes caught Shane's every once in a while, and I thought I detected a twinge of envy in his eyes. I would have preferred dancing with Shane instead of Lance, but propriety would not allow that. After the dance finished, I made my toast. Instead of just leaving at that point as I had at the other Balls, I walked over to Shane and said, "I want to walk into the crowd down there."

Shane gave me a worried look, but did not hesitate to notify the network of my intent. Agents swung into action forming a protective barrier around me as I walked into the crowd to great applause. I had not done this at any of the other Balls, and wanted to make a special gesture at this one. I shook hands, posed for a few pictures, and even got hugged by one bold guy who almost got knocked to the floor for his efforts by the agents. All the time, Shane had one hand inside the back of my pants that would have prevented anyone from pulling me into the crowd. It also felt good having Shane's hand where it was, I thought to myself. Finally after almost forty minutes with the gay community, I signaled that I was ready to leave. Orders were given, and I was escorted out of the hotel and into Limo One.

We arrived back at the White House at 3:32 and everyone was obviously tired, including Shane. As the detail brought me into the White House, I turned to them and said, "Thank you, ladies and gentlemen, for a job well done. I appreciate your service and look forward to a good working relationship with all of you. I'm sorry to have kept you up so late. Get some rest, and good night."

Shane and a second agent walked me to the elevator and we rode to the second floor in silence. My head was spinning from all the music, toasts, and sheer adulation that had been heaped upon me by the crowd.

At my bedroom door, Shane said goodnight, and informed me that Agent Harris would be on duty outside my bedroom tonight. I said thank you and good night to both and entered the sanctuary of my room. I quickly stripped off all of my clothes and leaped into bed naked, hoping no phone would ring until at least ten o'clock in the morning. I slept well.

CHAPTER 6
AND SO IT BEGINS...

My valet awoke me at 10:00 A.M. even though I could have slept for a couple more hours. I got out of bed, put on a robe and hit the shower. I spent a good fifteen minutes under the 'rain maker' shower heads and got out invigorated. Looking at myself in the mirror, I smiled at what I saw. I was thirty-eight years old, the youngest man ever to have been elected President, in good shape, light brown hair that was thick and shiny, with blue eyes. I had the good fortune to be slightly bettered endowed than most men, and was pleased by everything that I saw except my pecs. I needed to work on them a bit.

I put on my favorite underwear brand, Calvin Klein boxer briefs, and got dressed in a dark blue suit. The clothes complemented my physical appearance and I left my room feeling very Presidential.

Outside my bedroom door, I found Shane on duty with a different agent than the one that was outside my door when I retired. I bid them both good morning and headed to the dining room where coffee and orange juice had already been poured.

"Good morning, Mr. President, how are you today?" asked Henry.

"I feel great, Henry, and yourself?"

Henry smiled at the question Scalia had never once asked. "I'm fine, Mr. President, and happy to be here to serve you. What may I bring you for breakfast this morning?"

"Henry, since this was a sleep-in day, and lunch is only a couple hours away, I'll pass on anything to eat, and just enjoy this wonderful smelling coffee."

"Yes, sir, the papers are behind you on the sideboard. Will you be coming to the residence for lunch?"

"No, Henry, could you notify the kitchen to simply make me a sandwich and send it to the Oval Office?"

"Of course, Mr. President. By the way sir, the arrangements are complete and your personal agent has moved his things into his room while you slept."

"Great, Henry, thank you."

I quickly scanned the morning papers while I drank my coffee. There was major coverage of all the Balls of course, and particular attention paid to the Gay Ball. The fact that I danced with Lance Bass on stage seemed to have the same newsworthiness as Nixon's trip to China. There were various photographs of me at the assorted Balls as well as my return to the White House.

I finished my coffee and headed to the Oval Office.

"Good morning, Mr. President," rang out every few feet as I made my way through the office part of the White House. The last greeting came from Mary, who said I looked tired. I thanked her for her observation, noting that she looked like she had worked all night. This comment brought about a smile and the reply, "In fact I did, and I still manage to look this good!"

As I sat down at the desk used by Kennedy, I found a folder with the Presidential seal in the middle of it, containing ten executive orders, and the daily intelligence-briefing book that gave me a worldview of hot spots as well as anything that affected U.S. interests. This of course included the situation with Syria and the potential nuclear problem facing the region.

The ten executive orders were the ones I told Scalia I would sign on the first day. The first order mandated a total elimination of any barrier to a civil servant advancing or receiving a security clearance because he or she was gay. This reversed an order issued under Scalia that had withheld certain security clearances from gay people on the grounds that gays could be blackmailed into betraying their country.

The simple fact of the matter was that in all the cases of betrayal by an American of his or her country, heterosexual personnel committed the recorded disloyal acts. No gay person had ever betrayed the United States, a fact conveniently overlooked by those dealing with security clearance issues as well as the entire right wing of the nation. I was ending this disparate treatment for at least as long as I was President.

While issuing this order would have no significant reaction, the next one was sure to make the right howl. I signed Executive Order number 2136, ordering the Defense Department to discharge any enlisted person or officer found to have committed either adultery or having sex outside the legal state of marriage. This policy was ordered to stay in effect as long as 'don't ask, don't tell' remained the law of the land. This of course applied to all branches of the military and gave 'shore leave' an entirely new meaning and not one greeted with good cheer by the Navy. Instead of searching for brothels in foreign ports, the Navy could now search for historical ruins.

If the right wing wanted to legislate sexual morality, then it should be done all the way. What was good for gay people was good for straight people. I smiled with delight as I signed my name to this order.

The third executive order added sexual orientation to the list of reasons that a person could seek asylum in the United States. While the issue had surfaced before, this order would give White House backing to this category of refugee.

The remainder of the orders dealt with a variety of issues including reinstating the ban on Arctic drilling for oil, re-banning snow mobiles in national parks, and removing all literature from national parks that asserted the formation of such places as the Grand Canyon by God a mere three or four thousand years ago, instead of the millions of years ago when they were actually formed. Scalia had moved the national I.Q. down thirty points with some of his orders and I was determined to reverse that trend. In a mere ten minutes, I reversed some of the damage done over eight years by Scalia.

I put the folder to the side where I knew Mary would pick it up within minutes and get the orders disseminated. Next, I had a meeting scheduled with Andy Carter, my Chief of Staff. Mary, who scooped up the folder and left the office, showed him in and asked if he wanted any coffee. He declined and the meeting began.

"Good morning, Mr. President, how are you today?"

"Fine, Andy, recovering from last night. What's the status on all Agency heads?"

"Sir, as of this morning, all cabinet level Secretaries have been confirmed and you have a full Cabinet waiting to meet with you in about ninety minutes in the cabinet room. We may, however, have a problem that is not insignificant. I have heard rumblings out of the Old Executive Office building this morning that the Vice-President is not happy. It seems he's having second thoughts serving as your number two since you're gay. I have no idea why he waited until after taking the Oath of Office to let his unhappiness express itself, but nonetheless this is what I hear."

"Well, I suppose if he had taken himself off the ticket after Gorski outed me, it might have caused the party to lose the White House and he didn't want that on his resume. It was after all only six weeks until the general election when this all came out. He knows that if he had thrown the election into the loss column, he would be finished in politics."

"What do you want to do about this?"

I pressed the intercom and Mary answered.

"Mary, tell the Vice-President that Andy and I wished to see him here in the Oval Office."

"Yes, Mr. President."

"Look, I don't intend to play games with this. If he doesn't want to be on the team, then he needs to get off. Otherwise, he needs to shut up and do the job that he was elected to do."

"But what will you do if he resigns?"

"Pick a Vice-President that I really want instead of one I had to pick to carry the South. He really would be doing me a favor by quitting. Sure, there will be press fallout over it, but in time, it will fade and the new Veep will be fully accepted just as Nelson Rockefeller was accepted after replacing Agnew."

A few more minutes passed when Mary announced that Barry Miller, the Vice-President, was outside the office. I told her to send him in.

"Good morning, Mr. President."

"Good morning, Barry, please sit down. Can I get you anything?"

"No, thank you."

"The reason I asked you to come over is that it is my understanding that you're not happy to be part of this Administration because I'm gay. Is that correct?"

"My God, are there no secrets in Washington? I only mentioned that to someone this morning! Actually, no, I'm not happy being your number two. I didn't want to jump the ticket less than six weeks before the election, as I knew that would throw things into chaos and hand the White House back to the Republicans. So I kept my mouth shut, and played the good soldier. I also didn't want to alienate the entire Democratic Party."

"That's fine, Barry, and I appreciate that. But why exactly can't you serve as Vice-President because I'm gay? I don't understand; please explain that part to me, what does my sexuality have to do with you serving your country?"

"I mean no offense, sir, but as Vice-President, when I travel I represent you as well as the United States. I am tasked with getting your bills through Congress, an agenda that I might have serious problems with and yet I must pursue their passage. The fact that you're gay reflects on me and this Administration, and I don't feel comfortable with that."

"Well, with all due respect to you Barry, that's a bunch of bullshit. You're not responsible for my sexual orientation, and in fact, it shouldn't even be an issue. Your duties are the same whether I'm gay, straight, or celibate. If you feel my identity reflects on you, it's because you allow it to. Okay, assuming I cannot change your mind about this, what is your intention?"

"Sir, this is very difficult for me, but I have here in my jacket a letter of resignation from the office of the Vice-President."

"When is it effective, and what reason did you give?"

"It is effective today, and I used personal reasons for the cause of the resignation."

"Barry, you didn't even bother to talk to me about this and you were just planning on what? Walking in here and laying that on me without any notice? I expected more from you than that."

"I'm sorry, Mr. President, if I've disappointed you, but I feel I must do this."

"Your letter of resignation is accepted at once. Mary, would you come in here please?"

"Yes, sir?"

"Mary, the Vice-President has just resigned. Will you tell Jane to schedule a press conference in one hour, and call a top staff meeting in thirty minutes?"

"Anything else, sir?"

"Yes, make all the appropriate notifications internally that Mr. Miller is no longer a Government official."

Mary turned and left the office. The now former Vice-President stood up, apologized once more, and left the Oval Office.

"Andy, I want all of his security passes and clearances cancelled immediately. Please do that, and then meet me in the cabinet room."

Incredible, I thought to myself. Here I am in my first full day as President, and already I have a resignation and from the Vice-President no less! Was this a harbinger of things to come? Was it really going to be this tough being a President who happened to be gay?

Things began to move at lightning speed to signal the end of the Vice-President. Speechwriters were writing, security officials were busy canceling clearances, and my press spokesman was arranging the press conference that would take place so that I could announce to the country that they would have a new Vice-President.

Exactly thirty minutes after giving Mary the news, I walked into my meeting with White House staff that consisted of my top aides. Assembled in the room were eight people, all of whom I could not do without. Each person had a worried expression on their face, as they already knew the news that would be announced to the world shortly.

"Good morning, everyone. Well, I knew we would have days like this, but what I didn't know was that on day two, we would be having one of them. As you've all heard, Barry Miller has resigned. Your top task for me is to put together a very short list of replacement candidates as quickly as you can. Concentrate on experience, intelligence and party loyalty. Remember, the person you and I choose could one day have to take over as President. Let me see your list by ten o'clock tonight. Any questions?"

"One, sir. Are women on or off the list?"

"If she fits the characteristics that I just outlined, she's on the list." I waited a moment to see if anyone else had any questions. "Nothing further?" I verified. "Okay, get to work and get me that list."

I had time for a cup of coffee before the press conference and I took advantage of the few minutes I had to myself. I asked Shane to come into the Oval Office and sit down.

"Guess you heard what's going on?"

"Oh yeah, in fact, Miller is already gone from the OEB."

"What kind of list is an OEB?"

"It's not a list, sir; it stands for the Old Executive Office Building. He wasted no time in packing a single brief case that was inspected by the Secret Service, and leaving by private car. Apparently, he headed for Capitol Hill."

"Well, I'm about to announce the news via a press conference. What a day, and it isn't even noon yet! Are you all settled in at least in your new room?"

"Yes, sir, all in and unpacked. You're right, it is kind of lonely up there when you are just by yourself, and I understand how you felt now when you asked me to move in here."

"I'm sure it will be nice having you here, Shane."

The phone buzzed, and Mary announced, "Mr. President, you are due in the Press room in two minutes."

"Let's get this over with, shall we?"

As my Press Secretary introduced me, I walked onto the podium to the sight of camera flashes and no other sounds.

"Ladies and gentlemen, I have a statement to read. I will not be taking any questions afterwards, so please hold your questions.

"The Vice-President of the United States, Barry Miller, citing personal reasons, submitted his letter of resignation at twelve noon today, and I have accepted it. Mr. Miller has already departed from the White House grounds and is now a private citizen.

"My staff is already forming a short list of potential replacements for Mr. Miller and I expect to quickly select the best-qualified candidate to replace him. I hope to notify Congress and the American people who the new Vice-Presidential nominee will be by no later than Friday of this week. I ask that the Congress quickly confirm my choice for Vice-President so that we may move forward with the people's business. Thank you."

"Mr. President, Mr. President, one question please...."

I ignored the shouted questions and left the Press room, returning to the Oval office.

When I got there, I found my lunch waiting even though I didn't have much of an appetite. Mary came into the office and asked me if I was all right. She was concerned that I was being stressed out already and we hadn't even gotten through one full day yet.

"By the way, sir, I had the Chief Usher's office issue Shane passes for any of the personal things that you access as President so that he can use any facility while he's off duty that you can use. I assume that's okay with you?"

"Yes, thank you Mary, that's excellent. I want Shane to be as comfortable as possible while living here."

"You're rather fond of that young man, aren't you?

"Mary, what are you getting at?"

"Well, he is an extremely handsome young man who is also responsible for your protection. It would be natural if you felt more than the usual feelings for him," she said with a smile.

"Mary, we've known each other for enough years now that I know what you are getting at. Agent Thompson is merely staying close to me due to the attempt on the Hill. Nothing more."

"Okay sir, if that makes you feel better thinking that, then you go right ahead," she said as she swung around and left the Oval Office.

I was going have to be careful around her about Shane. She was too good at reading minds, and I didn't want her reading mine, I thought to myself as her response elicited a smile from me.

Later, as Shane and I were sitting in the living room of the residence, the phone buzzed.

"Mr. President, Andy Carter is here to see you," advised the Secret Service night duty officer.

"Fine, send him up."

Shane left the room as Andy entered.

"I take it that's my list?"

"Yes, Mr. President. I hope you'll be pleased with it since we didn't have a whole lot of time."

I took the folder and opened it to a short list of four candidates. Three were men and one woman. All four candidates met my requirements and now it became a matter of whom I could trust the most and who would get along with me. It appeared that there were no homophobes on the list, which wasn't necessarily a requirement prior to this morning. I could not afford another resignation because the person was 'uncomfortable' with me.

"Andy, these are all good people. I know Senator Gordon of course, and have met Governor Wilson a few times. The other two I know only by reputation. Who do you recommend?"

"Actually, sir, I might recommend General Kane as he brings a great deal of military experience to the position."

"While I totally respect his prior service to the country, I don't want a retired military officer in the Vice-Presidential slot. We already have one as Secretary of Defense, and I don't want this Administration to look like it is a retirement home for former flag and general staff officers. Would you see if you can get Governor Wilson on the phone right now?"

"Of course, sir."

"Governor's Mansion," answered the operator.

"Yes, Governor Wilson, please, this is the White House calling."

"And you expect me to just put you through because you say you're the White House? Well, at night, we become a chocolate factory, so the Governor is making chocolate and can't be disturbed."

Andy became visually flustered. "Madam, the President of the United States is waiting to speak to Governor Wilson. Please connect him with the Governor immediately, or have the Governor call the White House phone number for government officials and ask for the President."

"One moment sir, oh dear, I just checked our caller I.D. system, and I see it says U.S. Government. I apologize, sir, we get crank phone calls and I've become suspicious of anyone who says they are someone important trying to reach the Governor, especially at this hour of the day. I will put you through to the Governor's rooms immediately."

"Stupid woman thought it was a prank phone call. She's putting me through now."

"Governor Wilson speaking."

"Please hold for the President."

"Madam Governor, how are you this evening, sorry to be calling so late?"

"Fine, Mr. President, and I was reading this year's budget request, so I welcome the interruption. What can I do for you?"

"Victoria, I'd like you to come to the White House tomorrow to discuss becoming Vice-President of the United States. Would you be able to do that?"

"Mr. President, are you serious? Me, Vice-President, a Governor of the Virgin Islands?"

"Is there a reason I shouldn't consider you for the Vice-President's job?"

"No, sir, but I hope you can see why I am in shock. Hardly anyone even knows I'm alive down here in the Islands. Why me?"

"Because I might want to vacation in the Islands as President, and I believe you would know where all the good beaches and bars are?" I said with sardonic humor.

After she stopped laughing, she replied, "Mr. President, I would be honored to come to Washington to speak with you. Can I have my Chief of Staff work out all the arrangements with someone on your end?"

"Yes, talk to Andy Carter, White House Chief of Staff. Call the White House switch board and ask them to put you through to him and he'll let me know. I look forward to seeing you tomorrow. And please, be my guest at the White House tomorrow night and fly back the next day?"

"I would be honored to do that, sir."

"Very well then, I'll see you tomorrow."

I hung up the phone and looked at Andy. "She will be the next Vice-President, no doubt in my mind about it. She'll be here tomorrow, probably early afternoon. Have an Air Force plane pick her up and bring her into Andrews, and then quietly here to the White House."

"Very well, sir. Do you know how she is on the gay issue?"

"Her younger brother is gay. So, I think there will be no issues there."

"Fine, I'll let you know when she will be here as soon as I know."

Shane came in as Andy left. He didn't ask me about the business that had brought Carter to my private residence this late in the day.

"We'll have a guest tomorrow night staying in the Lincoln bedroom. Governor Wilson of the Virgin Islands will be here to talk to me about taking Miller's place."

"Interesting choice. A gay President and a woman Vice-President, the right wing will never recover from all this," he said with a laugh.

"They'll just have to get over it, or die with it on their minds," I responded with a smile.

"God, my back and neck aches from the tension today. It's too late to ask the Navy people to give me a massage, so I'll just have to live with it."

Shane smiled, "Not if you don't want to. I've been told I give excellent massages and would be happy to show you that the people who said that were correct."

I felt myself begin to grow stiff in my shorts just thinking about Shane handling my body. It was going to happen sooner or later, so why not tonight?

"I'm going to take you up on that offer. Shall we go into my bedroom?"

"Lead the way."

"Oh, what about the agent on duty outside my door?"

"Mr. President, one thing you don't know about this house is that the bookcase in your room swings out and leads into a very narrow passage that connects to the bedroom I now occupy. This was built when the White House was refurbished during the Truman years, and enabled the President to pass unseen into the bedroom used sometimes by his wife, Bess. John Kennedy used the passage frequently for other reasons. Go in, and I'll join you in just a few minutes, but make sure you pull out the book on the top left hand side of the shelf, titled 'War and Peace'. That will allow the case to be opened from the other side."

"God bless Harry Truman! See you shortly."

I said goodnight to the agent outside my room and entered. I took off all my clothes except my boxer briefs, and put on a robe that bore the Presidential Seal. I pulled out 'War and Peace' and heard a distinctive 'click' when the book went as far as it could. I sat down on the sofa, nervous as a schoolgirl. How far was I willing to let it go should things get heated between us? Could I in fact control my urges?

The sound of another click coming from the bookcase and the sight of it opening outwards broke my train of thought. Shane came through the opening dressed only in gym shorts and socks with a Secret Service t-shirt on. He looked beautiful in the reduced light of the bedroom. It was kind of romantic, like my lover was sneaking into my arms to keep polite society ignorant of my affair.

Before I could censor my words, I said, "You look sexy as hell."

"You don't look bad yourself for a Chief Executive dressed in a bathrobe," he said with a smile that could melt ice.

I got up and walked over to him and gave way to my urge to take him in my arms and hug him. We stood like that for several moments when my hands fell down onto his ass. He did not move them or object. Running my hands up and down the rock firmness of each cheek, I grew hard beneath my robe, as did Shane. I released my embrace and kissed him on the lips. As I did, he forced his tongue into my mouth and I gave way to its probing. Here I stood in the President's bedroom, French kissing one of my Secret Service agents. I was in a daze and my desire rose to the heights of irresistibility. I pulled Shane over to the bed and looked into his eyes, silently asking him if he wanted to make love without ever uttering a single word. I got the response that I had hoped for. Looking at the bulge jutting forth from Shane's crotch, my mouth watered.

"We have to be careful or the agent outside the door will hear us," I whispered.

"When you go to bed for good at night, the agent moves down the hallway away from your bedroom door and takes his post across from the elevator. Unless we begin to practically shout, he won't hear anything."

Keeping that in mind, my eyes returned to the prize before me. I reached out and ran my hand over the length of Shane's erection and underneath to hold his balls. He was hard and I could not wait any longer as I reached back up to the waistband of his shorts, pulling them down to expose a bright pair of white jockey shorts. His cock looked even bigger now with just one layer of clothing between it and freedom. I quickly pulled his shorts down and his cock sprang out at me. He was beautiful. His cock and low hanging full balls were in perfect harmony with his above average body. He was cut and had his pubic hair trimmed closely.

I pulled on Shane's cock to bring him closer to the bed and looked up at him.

"Are you sure you are all right with crossing this line?"

He did not answer. Instead he pushed his hips out and slipped the head of his cock into my mouth where I eagerly began to suck. He smelled sweet and tasted wonderful. I tried to go all the way down on him, but could not take the last inch or so given how thick he was at the base. I breathed in the scent of man and began to suck his cock with long strokes of my mouth. I played with his balls with my right hand as I caressed his marble-like ass with my other hand.

Shane pulled out of my mouth and pulled me to my feet. He undid my robe and pushed it off my shoulders and down onto the floor. His hand then went to my basket and began to fondle my cock and balls. I was already hard and so he stroked my cock through my shorts. I kissed him deeply, strong feelings of passion building as he shoved my shorts down my legs and onto the floor using only his one hand and leg. We now both stood naked, embraced in each other's arms, our hard-ons touching and rubbing against one another.

Shane lowered me onto the bed, lifting my legs up and on the end of the bed as he began to straddle my chest. Bending over, he licked each of my nipples making them hard and responsive as he flicked them. I had to bite my tongue to keep from moaning from the pleasure he was giving me. Shane worked his way down my chest, stomach, and finally to my cock. He continued to flick his tongue around the head of my cock and along the shaft until he reached my balls. There he ran his tongue over each one, lightly sucking on them, teasing them, and taking each ball one at a time into his mouth. He ran his tongue back up my shaft until he reached my head.

Shane took my cock into his mouth and began to slowly go down on me. He took at least a minute to go all the way down, taking the entire seven inches into his mouth and throat, slowly sucking my cock with the expertise of a man trained in the oral arts by some cock-sucking master of the Far East. I was writhing in bed, tossing my head back and forth, my ass cheeks clenching and unclenching. Shane saw my balls begin to tighten up and rise towards the base of my cock and knew that was the warning sign that I was drawing close to an end.

He released my cock and rolled over onto his back allowing me to cool down a bit. As I gazed at his perfect body, I was considerably impressed by the contour of his pectoral muscles, and the way his chest dipped down from them and rose slightly before dropping off onto his stomach. Then he rose again at his crotch where he was hung with about eight gorgeous inches and nice medium size balls. His thighs and legs were well muscled and in proportion. This was a man with all the right genes.

When I felt myself fully under control again, I rolled over on my side and began to move my hand up and down Shane's body. I saw goose bumps rise up all over his skin even though the light was dim and the flicker of the fire danced across his nakedness. Lowering my lips to his left nipple, I sucked on it lightly, teasing it to make it grow and become hard once again. I ran my tongue over Shane's chest relishing every inch. Kissing his ear, I whispered, "Turn over."

As the fullness of Shane's ass came into view, I literally gasped at its sheer unadulterated male beauty. His ass would make Michelangelo's David cry with jealousy. It rose up from his lower back like a road rising to meet Mount McKinley. He had the perfect curve that gave the original meaning to the term 'bubble butt'. His cheeks cascaded down onto his upper thighs leaving behind a thing of sheer beauty. A light coating of fuzz covered most of his posterior and I found myself drawn to it. I moved my head towards his ass and allowed my tongue to wash over his beauty, eliciting little moans from deep within him. I covered every square inch with kisses intermingled with a tongue bath, paying attention to every little bit. I wanted to dive into the crevice between his cheeks, but didn't know yet if he would enjoy that, so I didn't. Besides, I wanted to save something for the next time, assuming there was one.

I also wanted to engage in some good old-fashioned butt fucking, but once again, I did not want to go for something that Shane had not indicated that he wanted. I was determined to be a considerate lover to this beautiful man, the least he deserved in giving himself to me in this most intimate way. Of course, I didn't know really if I wanted to be top or bottom in that act, as Shane brought out different emotions in me than most men did. I was always the top before, but I could see the pleasure in giving Shane my ass to do with as he pleased.

"That was nice, sir, I really enjoyed that. You have a gifted tongue," he said with a smile. "Can we lay here in each other's arms for a bit before we finish each other?"

"First of all, after you've had your cock stuffed into my mouth and vice-versa, I think it almost mandatory that you call me David, and not sir or, God forbid, Mr. President. As to your question, yes, we can lie here before I finish sucking your beautiful cock off for you."

The phone rang as we lay together, and I moved out of Shane's arms to answer it. "President Windsor."

"Andy, Mr. President, I thought you would want to know that Vicky will be here by 11 A.M. and will be staying the night as your guest. I left a message for Mary to clear anything you have for 11:30 so you can meet after she freshens up a bit. Are those arrangements okay, sir?"

"Yes, Andy, they're fine, thank you for notifying me. Now, I'm off to sleep."

"Good night, Mr. President."

Before I could hang up the phone, Shane had once again taken my cock into his mouth and was sucking it hard. His head pumped my cock like a piston. I sank back into the pillows of the Presidential bed while my Secret Service agent, and now friend and soon-to-be lover, gave me fantastic head. As I felt myself begin to build to a climax, I warned Shane to get off before I did. Instead of pulling off, he sucked harder and deeper, taking my full load down this throat, making sure not to miss a single drop. He literally sucked my balls dry, as I covered my face with a pillow to muffle the sounds of ecstasy that his sucking evoked. As my dick began to soften, he finally let it plop out onto my stomach, looking up at me and smiling as I uncovered my face and let out a deep sigh of contentment.

"You give fantastic head, Shane," I said, uttering words I was sure had never been heard in this room before.

"So, you like my work?" he asked with a chuckle.

"Like everything else you do, my friend, you suck cock perfectly. You can actually teach me a thing or two about how to properly suck a dick dry," I replied with a smile.

"Shall we begin now?"

"By all means, how do you want it?"

"Lie on your back and bring your head over to the edge of the bed."

I did as I was ordered, and found myself staring up into the head of Shane's cock, which was pushed down towards my nose.

"Now open your mouth wide and move your head just over the edge of the bed."

I complied and Shane slipped his cock into my mouth from above me, allowing him to insert his entire length into my mouth and down my throat. He began to rock back and forth, fucking my throat. As I looked up, I watched his balls swing to and fro with every inbound stroke. I also had the advantage of being able to admire his ass and its beautiful curve as he continued to fuck my mouth. The pace of his face fucking picked up and after about six or seven minutes, I saw his balls begin to tighten and climb up into his scrotum. I guessed that he was about to come, particularly when I felt him begin to withdraw his beauty of a dick. Placing both hands on his ass, I prevented him from pulling out, instead pushing him deep into my throat. He understood that I wanted to take his load.

After about another dozen thrusts of his hips, I felt his cock enlarge slightly, hot streams of come hitting the back of my mouth, the back of my throat, and I had all I could do to swallow to keep up with the very large load that Shane was putting out. In fact, I gagged twice, not able to swallow as fast as he was coming. Finally, his thrusts slowed and now I had only a slight new burst of come every few seconds until no more came forth from his cock. As he pulled his tool out of my mouth, I tasted a combination of salt and sweetness left by his voluminous orgasm. I rather liked the taste. Shane's heavy cock flopped against my forehead as he rested for a moment after climaxing so hard. I ran my tongue out and licked the slit in his head for that last drop of nectar.

I was once again fully erect from the face fucking I had just taken and I began to jerk off when Shane bent back over me and went down on me again. I whispered that it was not necessary, that I had just become horny again from his fucking my face. He didn't say a word; he just worked my cock while his own cock hung over my face. I thought what the hell, and began to suck his prick once again. We began to sixty-nine in earnest when we realized that we both wanted to come again. We vigorously sucked each other's cock until we both busted another nut into our mouths after about ten minutes of continuous sucking. When we had finished, Shane collapsed on top of me and we rolled onto the bed exhausted from our lovemaking. I kissed him one more time on the lips and said, "Thank you. You have no idea how much I needed that or how much I enjoyed the fact that it was you I was making it with."

"You don't need any lessons in the art of taking a cock. You were great, but I must tell you, I trapped you into a second load," he said smiling.

I had no idea what he was talking about. "Huh?"

"By my fucking your face the way I did, you got to watch my cock, balls and ass in motion. I knew you'd be horny again after all that and I was right. We got off twice because of that position."

"You dirty dog, you're right, you are one hot boy in the sack and I'm never going to complain about tricks like that."

"If we ever make love again, maybe you would be willing to try the other side of the coin?"

"You mean butt fucking?"

"Yeah, I mean butt fucking, like two dogs in heat!" he said with an evil smile.

"I'll see if you're a good boy or not, and if you are, maybe I'll fuck your tight beautiful ass for you."

"Ha, I'm the top here, but since you're the boss, maybe I'll take it in the ass for you," he said, once again smiling.

"I wish you could sleep with me tonight. This has been a wonderful experience and not just because I got to suck a nice cock and get blown myself. I really like you, and I liked pleasing you, even if I hadn't received anything in return."

"That's never going to happen. You keep telling me I'm hot; have you looked in the mirror lately? Men like you don't come along every day, y'know, and when they do, and you like them on top of their looks, it's a good day for all. But I'd better get going, we both need sleep, and neither one of us will get any if I stay here."

"Good night, Shane, and thank you," I said, kissing him and grabbing his dick one last time.

Watching Shane leave my room naked to go to his room through the passageway, I thought to myself how much I really did like this man. I might even be able to fall in love with him. Was that possible as President? Could I have a love life in addition to a sex life? Or was I hoping for too much?

CHAPTER 7
THE ISLANDS ARE BEAUTIFUL THIS TIME OF THE YEAR

James woke me up at 7 A.M. and had already laid out a suit for me to wear for the day. The Governor of the Virgin Islands and maybe the next Vice- President of the United States was due in just four hours and I had a lot of work to do before she arrived.

I skipped breakfast and had Henry send coffee to the Oval Office. I was in an incredibly good mood from the events of last night. Not only had I gotten sex, but great sex with someone that really attracted me How would Shane act around me now? Would it be awkward?

Shane was his usual professional self who once again looked stunning in one of his suits. I smiled at him as I entered the Oval Office and he took up his post outside the door. I had much to do today of great importance and had to get my mind off Shane's body.

Andy Carter and one of the legislative aides came into the office about five minutes after I arrived. This was a meeting to begin our legislative agenda and we already knew getting some of our programs through would be difficult. I pushed gay agenda items halfway down on the list to give the right wing one less target to shoot at as I began. I learned from Bill Clinton's mistakes, remembering that soon after taking office, he began with an attempt to fulfill his campaign promises to the gay community and failed at most of them. I was determined to take a more calculated and thought-out approach to these issues.

I intended to shock Congress with the unexpected submission of proposed legislation tightening certain regulation on mine safety. Our nation's miners were protected by the Mine Safety and Health Act of 1966, which was supposed to insure that safety was the number one concern of coalmine owners. The Act was a great improvement over regulations previously in place but it had holes.

One such hole was with the imposition of fines for violation of the Act. There was very little uniformity in the amounts of fines imposed as they depended ultimately on administrative law judges to set final amounts. More times than not, fines went uncollected from the mine owners, making the regulations far less critical to the proper operation of coalmines.

One simple amendment to the penalty phase of the process would go a long way to correcting these problems. I would propose to issue mandatory minimum penalties for certain 'life critical' violations with the authority to shut the mine down for non-payment of those fines. Civil penalties were of no use if there was no effective enforcement tool to collect the penalties issued against mine owners. The authority to close a mine would rest with the Assistant Secretary of MSHA, the mine safety agency, which reported to the Secretary of Labor, and not with any administrative law judge. I would take great care in selecting the new head of MSHA within the next few weeks. All an owner had to do to reopen a mine was correct the deficiency that caused the violation, and pay the fine. The owner was free to appeal the fines, but their mine would remain closed until such time as the fine was paid.

This policy would cease the current methods that mine operators used to delay and often never pay the penalties imposed upon them, thus failing to act as a deterrent to the safe operation of mines. The mine owners would not be happy with this proposed change and would fight it tooth and nail. Let them; the American worker was far more important.

The second of the proposed legislative initiatives would be the imposition of heavy taxes on corporations that shipped American jobs overseas. This now all too common operational norm was costing America not only skilled jobs, but semi-skilled ones as well. Entire call centers were being sent to India, thus depriving the American jobs market of jobs that people who were semi-skilled could easily be trained to do while receiving a decent wage. Computer companies, banks, and many corporations that had customer service phone centers were depleting America of jobs that were essential to many people. They did this of course to save money but with the imposition of heavy taxes that would be funneled into the unemployment insurance system, their incentive would drop dramatically and America might recover tens of thousands of jobs that had been lost to low cost labor markets overseas.

I knew that in proposing this legislation, I would cause another furor similar to the mine legislation, but I had been elected on a promise to restore fairness to the working class of people in America. This left the third leg of this initial legislative package: taxes.

I intended to propose a revamping of the tax code to restore fairness and badly needed income to the common working person whose wages had been siphoned off by an unfair tax system. I was proposing that taxes on those who made in excess of one million dollars a year be increased by seven percent, while those making less than fifty thousand a year would be cut by ten percent.

I also intended to propose a national sales tax of two percent on all purchases over one thousand dollars, not including automobiles, which would remain unaffected by this proposal. In addition, a flat tax of one hundred dollars on all sales and purchases of real estate would be implemented. This tax would only affect those who could afford to buy property but not those who were too poor to be able to make this kind of purchase and were forced to live in apartments. This tax was not high enough to be able to affect whether a person bought or sold real estate but would generate needed revenue, which would be funneled into a national program to rebuild the nation's infrastructure. America's bridge and road system was nearing collapse due to neglect and lack of funding by the states. Using this tax source would spread the cost of these repairs throughout the country, which would benefit the entire nation.

"Okay, let's get this written up as proposed legislation, let me review it, and get it up to the Hill as soon as possible. The second round of proposals will begin to deal with the gay community."

"Yes, Mr. President," replied Andy.

Mary knocked on the door and came in. "Mr. President, General Sinclair is on the telephone and says it's urgent."

"My first call from the Chairman of the Joint Chiefs, this should be interesting. Thank you, Joseph, you may go and get started on all that," I said to the aide before picking up the phone.

"President Windsor."

"Mr. President, General Sinclair here. I need to advise you that approximately thirty minutes ago, Iranian speedboats attacked the USS Dillon while she was on routine patrol in the Gulf, killing two seamen before the Dillon destroyed two of the three attacking boats. The third speedboat managed to escape while losing only one member of its crew."

"I'm sorry to hear about the loss of our men, General. Does the Pentagon have any reason for the attack?"

"Sir, the Iranians have been trying to extend their territorial control of the waterways of that area far beyond what is normal, for some time now. We believe this risky incident was an attempt to make the U.S. back down and give in to their demands."

"We of course will do no such thing, General. What are the current rules of engagement for our ships operating in those waters?"

"Sir, they are to open fire only upon being fired upon. This allowed the speedboats to get in fairly close, permitting them to use shoulder launched missiles, which is what led to the death of the seamen."

"I understand, General. Issue a new rule of engagement for all U.S. ships operating in those waters. All Iranian patrol boats are to be considered hostile, and will be fired upon and sunk before they can get close enough to our vessels to cause any damage to crew or vessel. This is not permission to pursue speedboats that are not approaching our vessels, General, but only those whose intent can be assumed to be hostile to our interests. Any questions?"

"No, sir, your orders are clear. I will see that this change goes out within the next ten minutes."

"Very good, General, please keep me informed of events in the Gulf." I hung up the phone.

"Andy, the Iranians are acting up once again. I came into office this week trying to be a President of peace, and before I can even start, our enemies have attempted to provoke me. I want a total review of all operational orders covering our military forces in the Gulf. These days, it is totally insane to wait until we have lost personnel before defending ourselves. We must strike a balance between passivity and overt aggression."

"Yes sir, I will get on it right away."

The intercom rang and Mary advised me that the Governor of the Virgin Islands had arrived a little early at the White House.

"Have her come right in, I've finished up the legislative business."

The door to the Oval Office opened to admit Governor Wilson. She was beautiful in her manner, appearance and charm. She wore a deep purple dress, with a long necklace made from real pearls. She stood about five foot nine, and weighed about 145 pounds.

"Good morning, Mr. President, thank you for inviting me to the White House."

"Welcome, Madam Governor, it's a pleasure to have you here with us. I hope your trip was bearable?"

"It was fine, sir; the Air Force treated me like I was royalty. Not bad flying with your own jet available to you."

"Yes, well, I haven't used my 'own' jet yet, but I hear it's rather nice," I said with a smile.

"Mr. President, I know you said you wanted me here to discuss becoming your Vice-President, but have you considered all of the far more talented and experienced people ahead of me? I am Governor of islands that are not even a state and you wish to consider me?"

"Vicky, I look for certain things that are far more important than where a candidate comes from, or how important the office is that is held by the candidate. You fit the principal criteria for this most important post. You are intelligent, creative, intuitive, and loyal to the party. You are also someone who I could rest easy at night knowing is but a heartbeat away from this office. There has already been one attempt on my life before I was even sworn in, and the likelihood of another attempt is high. I have complete confidence in you should you need to take over as President. Now, because of the reason that Miller resigned, I must ask any potential replacement this. Do you have a problem with me being gay?"

"Mr. President, the most important person in my life is gay: my son. Not only that, but my brother is also gay. I have long ago adjusted to the fact that there are people in this life who are born gay, and it is as normal as being born heterosexual. In the seventeen years that my son has been alive, I have learned that his sexuality bears no relationship to the things that he will accomplish in life. When you were elected to this office, Darren truly began to believe that he could become anything. You've given hope to my son, and millions like him, that being gay is not a curse, but can be a great blessing. So, the easy answer to your question, Mr. President, is no, your being gay does not give me reasons to be concerned."

"I didn't know your son was gay, and I would have believed your answer regardless. How do the other kids treat him?"

"Oh, he runs into the occasional bully, but he takes far more guff for being the Governor's son than he does for being gay."

"Well, one thing I can assure you of; if you become Vice-President, he will never have to worry about such a thing as a bully again. There will be a Secret Service agent with him most of the time, including school. I of course would want only the best for him as he grows into adulthood. Your office can give him advantages that he might not have otherwise."

"Yes, but regardless of my office, neither you nor I can get him into a military academy, now can we?"

"No, not at the present time. But I intend to do all I can to get rid of that asinine policy, 'don't ask, don't tell'. Would you like to help me do that?"

"Without question, sir."

"The FBI is currently doing a quick background on you that would suffice to be able to nominate you while the extended check goes on. Would you accept an offer of becoming my Vice-President?"

"Yes, sir, I would."

"I can't do anything formally with you until that initial check comes back. I hope to have it shortly, possibly while you're here in Washington. Please don't discuss this with anyone until it becomes official."

"Do I understand you correctly that you are intending to offer me the job?"

"You understand me correctly, Madam Governor."

"What should I do until you can 'pop' the question?"

"Until then, consider yourself both a guest of the White House and a tourist free to go anywhere you like in Washington, providing that you agree to a security presence."

"Yes, of course."

"Mary, will you ask the head of the White House Secret Service detail to join us?" I asked on the intercom.

"Yes, Mr. President."

"Would you like anything to drink while we wait?"

"No, thank you sir. I'm frankly too nervous at the moment."

Mary opened the door and showed the SAC into the Oval Office.

"Yes, Mr. President, what can I do for you?"

"This is Governor Wilson as you already know undoubtedly. I intend to ask her to become the new Vice-President shortly. Would you assign to her appropriate agents as of now until either she is no longer a candidate, or her protection becomes permanent?"

"Yes, sir, I would be happy to do that."

"Also, should she in fact become Vice-President, she has a seventeen year old son, who I want protected all the time, just as if he was the son of the President, understood?"

"Yes, sir, in fact, I can send a couple of agents to secure him now in the Virgin Islands if you'd like."

"Unless the Governor objects, that would be excellent."

"No objection here, and thank you, Mr. President, for that courtesy."

"Mary, please come here."

The door opened and Mary quickly appeared. "Yes, sir?"

"Mary, will you have the usher show the Governor to the Lincoln bedroom and where things are so she's comfortable the rest of the day and night?"

"Of course, sir. This way, Governor."

"Until we speak again, Vicky," I said as I extended my hand to her.

I punched the button on the phone that connected me with the Chief of Staff.

"Yes, sir?"

"Andy, I'm going to nominate Victoria Wilson for Vice-President. Would you prepare the paperwork for Congress? I'm waiting for the initial FBI clearance to come back so I can formally offer her the position. But I have no doubt she will pass, so let's begin the work involved so we can move on to the things that we should be working on."

"Right away, sir."

AS the governor left the White House grounds for the first time as potential Vice-President, she decided to go to the Lincoln Memorial where she'd found inspiration on her last trip to Washington as candidate for governor. As she got out of the car, two members of the press ran up to her shouting questions as to why she was in Washington.

"Oh, I'm here to pay a visit to our nation's monuments and to remember all of the sacrifices made by our forefathers to make this country what it is today. From here, I want to see the World War Two monument which I haven't seen yet."

"Madam Governor, there's a rumor in Washington that you are staying at the White House in order to discuss the job of being Vice-President, would you comment on that?"

"Even though the Islands are beautiful this time of the year, I wanted to see the beauty of Washington. Now if you will excuse me, President Lincoln is waiting for me."

CHAPTER 8
NUCLEAR DIPLOMACY

T he next morning, I was told that Governor Wilson had passed her initial security clearance and was therefore eligible to be nominated for Vice-President. She arrived at the Oval Office at 9:45 A.M. and joined me for coffee.

"Good morning, Governor, did you sleep well in the Lincoln bedroom?"

"Oh yes, I thoroughly enjoyed myself. It was a privilege to have been able to sleep in that room."

"Outstanding. Madam Governor, I would formally like to offer you the office of Vice-President of the United States. Do you accept the nomination?"

"Mr. President, I accept. I will serve the American people, you, and the party to the best of my ability. Thank you for the great honor and confidence that you have shown me by this nomination."

"Excellent. I've scheduled a press conference for 11:00 A.M. this morning to announce to the nation that your name will be going to the Hill for what I hope will be a quick confirmation, so you can begin your duties as soon as you can relocate from the Islands to Washington. The Secret Service has already been notified, and your son is under full protection as we speak. He apparently thinks it's 'neat' to have bodyguards."

"Yeah, until he wants to go on a date!"

We both broke out laughing at the humor involved but also with some sympathy for the young man as he learned to live in a fish bowl. Life was going to change greatly for the Wilson family.

At 11:00, I held the press conference to announce Wilson's nomination. I then let her have the podium to face the White House press corps for the first time. Governor Wilson handled herself with great aplomb and I rather enjoyed watching her fence with the lions of the press. After it was over, the governor paid a quick visit to Capitol Hill to meet with both the Senate Majority Leader and minority leaders who would be responsible for moving her nomination through the confirmation process. After finishing there, she left for Andrews and flew back to the Virgin Islands to a waiting press corps of her own.

At 2:35 that afternoon, I received an urgent phone call from the signal corps that I was needed in the situation room of the White House. This was the set of rooms that were buried 127 feet below the White House that were reached by a single elevator restricted to the President and authorized military personnel only along with anyone cleared by the president. I told Shane where I needed to go and we quickly moved from the public rooms of the White House to the appropriate elevator in a restricted area. A Marine guard punched the codes into the panel that allowed the elevator to descend to the waiting chamber below.

When the doors opened, I stepped out into a room that had United States Marines on guard who sprang to attention and escorted me through a set of double doors, leading to yet another door that when opened, allowed access to the situation room.

This was a room reserved for the handling of military crises along with any other national emergency. On the walls were various LCD monitors that carried world maps indicating U.S. and other countries' military presence. There was a map of Syria on the center monitor hanging directly opposite my chair at the conference table. On the table were a series of telephones that connected military personnel to various branches of the military as well as the Pentagon, the State Department, Defense Department, and the Department of Justice. Special phones also went to the FBI, CIA, NSA, and certain key foreign government leaders.

I was the last person to arrive as there were duty officers already representing the various agencies involved. Everyone stood up when I entered the room, and I told everyone to sit down and begin the briefing.

General Gordon of the NSA outlined the situation.

"Mr. President, we have intelligence indicating that the Syrians are preparing to threaten the use of one of their nuclear weapons on Israel to force them into conceding all lands won in the June 1967 war, as well as relinquishing all Palestinian lands on the West Bank. We believe that the Syrians have in fact two nuclear weapons sold to them by the Russians, and not one as previously believed. Further, we have learned that this plan has the blessing of both the Iranians and the Saudis. We believe the use of this threat is imminent."

"Does this have anything to do with the attack on the Dillon in the Gulf?"

"Yes, sir, we believe that the Iranians were testing our resolve to fight back as one way of judging our tenacity. Plainly, they were testing you, sir."

"Admiral Hancock, the new rules of engagement are in force?"

"Yes, Mr. President, as you ordered. There have been no new probes of our ships' defenses since the incident."

"Does Israel know of this pending threat, and if so, what are they doing in response?"

"Yes sir, they know. In fact, they have put their own nuclear forces on full alert. This could get very messy, very quickly, and involve the entire Middle East."

"Are we staying in close contact with the Israelis so they don't do anything stupid?"

"Yes sir, we are trying to keep them calm."

As I was studying one of the maps on display, a phone rang in front of the Admiral. He answered it and went slightly pale. He mumbled something and hung up.

"Mr. President, a report has just come in that the Nimitz is being shadowed by what is believed to be an Iranian submarine. Our carrier is doing twenty knots in calm seas headed for the Strait of Hormuz. The sub fails to answer any attempt at radio contact."

"The damn Iranians have a sub force? How the hell is that even possible?"

"The Russians sold them one or two of their diesel subs about three years ago. This is the first time one has come even close to one of our ships."

"How soon before the Nimitz is in the straits?"

The Admiral picked up his phone and asked that question.

"Fifty minutes, Mr. President."

"Bring up the map of that area showing the Nimitz."

A second later, a very detailed map of the entire area of the strait was on the central monitor. It was obvious that when a ship passed through that point, they were in effect in a bottleneck. The Iranians could attack from land as well as from under the sea. Our carrier would also be vulnerable to attack by air.

"Comments or suggestions, gentlemen?"

"Sir, the Nimitz will be at risk under the current conditions. We can either alter course and avoid going through the straits or take offensive actions."

"What kind of offensive action, Admiral?"

"We could initiate anti-sub warfare and attempt to sink the Iranian sub, as well as launch air combat patrols."

"Has the sub taken any overt hostile maneuvers that you are aware of, Admiral?"

"No, sir, they are just shadowing the Nimitz."

"What if we launch air patrols but not initiate action against the sub?"

"Mr. President, if we launch air operations against the Iranians, the sub will more than likely attack."

"Get me the President of Iran on the phone," I ordered my Air Force communications officer.

Two minutes later, I was informed that the Iranian president was on the line. I put him on speakerphone so everyone could hear.

"President Windsor here, are you there, Mr. President?"

"Yes, I am here. What is it that the great United States wants?"

"The United States wants you to order your sub that is following the USS Nimitz in the Gulf to cease its operations immediately and leave the area of the American ships."

"President Windsor, the Revolutionary Guard Naval forces are exercising their role for Iran in international waters and are not subject to your will, or did you forget that?"

"Mr. President, the United States military considers your sub a threat and it must be ordered to cease its current actions."

"And if the sub continues its present course, then what?"

"You, Mr. President, will be in the market for a replacement for that sub as it will be in pieces all over the bottom of the Gulf. Is that what you really want?"

"That would be an act of war and Iran would be entitled to defend itself including the firing of Sunburst anti-ship missiles that China has so kindly sold to us for defense against America. Is that what you really want?"

"Mr. President, your country has been itching for a major fight since 1979. I guess it's about time you got it. Can you hear me clearly, Mr. President? You are on speaker phone so that you can hear all of what I am about to say."

"Of course I can hear you."

"Good, because I don't want any of this to be a surprise to you. Admiral Stenchon, order the Nimitz to sink the Iranian submarine and to launch air combat patrols immediately. General Watson, have two B-52's take off immediately from the nearest Air Force base, loaded with bunker buster bombs, and target Iran's Parliament and Presidential residence. If any Sunburst missile is fired by any country in the Gulf towards our ships, give the go order for the B-52's to complete their mission."

"Yes, Mr. President," answered both officers.

"If I were you, Mr. President, I would either call off your sub at once, or get the hell out of Tehran."

"This is outrageous, you cannot attack our country, we will unleash the entire Muslim world on you!"

"That's your decision, Mr. President. Let's make a deal: you stop fucking with the U.S. and we will leave your pain in the ass country alone. As we say here in America, the ball's in your court."

I broke the connection with the Iranian president.

"How soon before the Nimitz commences anti-sub warfare?"

"I would say in just under five minutes," responded the Admiral.

"Get an update on that sub; see if it's changed its course and speed."

After another two minutes, I was told the sub had veered off course and was headed away from the Nimitz.

"Cancel the locate and sink order and recall the bombers if they've even gotten off the ground yet."

Both officers picked up their respective phones and issued the recall orders. I breathed a sigh of relief but then realized that the original problem that brought me to this bunker was still in play.

"Now, back to Syria. We can't allow them to use this threat and get away with it. We need diplomacy to handle this kind of a problem before Israel takes away our options. Major, get me the Syrian president on the phone.

It took over ten minutes before the phone contact was completed.

"Mr. President, the Syrian president on the phone."

"This is President Windsor, how are you Mr. President?"

"I am fine Mr. President, what can I do for you?"

"It is good to hear you are well. What you can do for me is to avert the destruction of the Middle East, are you interested in that goal?"

"What do you mean, sir?"

"President Assad, we are aware that it is Syria's plan to use the threat of nuclear war against Israel to achieve certain policy goals of Syria's and others in the Middle East. We know that you intend to make certain threats shortly. This will not be received well by Israel, and might very possibly lead to the destruction of Syria as well as the rest of your part of the world. I want to propose an immediate face-to-face conference involving Israel, the United States, Syria and the other Middle Eastern States. The attendees would all be the heads of state, no underlings. The goal of this conference would be once and for all to bring if not peace to the Middle East, then a method by which all parties concerned could co-exist. The alternative is death. What do you say?"

"Mr. President, I am shocked that you believe that Syria is about to take any action against Israel, by threat or force. Where do you get such information?"

"President Assad, if you intend to just play games then I will end this phone call and proceed to protect our interests in the region. Or you can drop the façade, and deal with this issue that is not going to go away – what's your choice, sir?"

There were several seconds of silence before Assad responded. "Very well, Mr. President. Let us meet face to face – where, when and who?"

"The who is the easy part. Syria, Israel, Saudi Arabia, Iran and Egypt. I propose to have the conference in Jordan if King Hussein agrees to be the host. As for when, within the next couple of weeks. Will that work?"

"I want Russia included as well."

"No. Russia has no role in the Middle East and hasn't with the exception of being an arms supplier to certain countries. They do not play a part in this and I will not have them extending their influence into a region that is already volatile enough as it is without them as part of the equation. That, as we say in America, is a deal breaker."

"Very well, Mr. President, have it your way on this point. I will instruct my Foreign Affairs Minister to begin the contacts. Will you contact Jordan?"

"Yes, today. As soon as I have an answer from the King, I will notify your people. I look forward to seeing you at this meeting and truly hope you approach this chance at peace with a serious heart."

"Until then, Mr. President, good day."

The connection was broken and the room was quiet while I thought.

"Get me King Hussein of Jordan."

While that was being accomplished, I rang Mary and told her to clear the rest of the day of all appointments except any to do with Governor Wilson. With all this going on, I wanted a Vice-President in place.

"Also, schedule a White House meeting with the Speaker of the House and the Senate Majority Leader for three o'clock this afternoon in the Oval Office. Just tell them that it has nothing to do with Wilson."

"Yes, Mr. President."

"Mr. President, King Hussein is apparently on a motorcycle somewhere in the Jordanian kingdom but they will track him down and call us when he can talk on a secure line."

"On a motorcycle? Somewhere in the kingdom? He obviously doesn't have the restriction of movement that I do. Very well, I'll be in the Oval Office or the residence."

I left the room the way I entered and was met by Shane's beautiful face once again. Seeing him never failed to put a smile on my face. I entered the elevator with four agents and proceeded to the White House level and my office. As I arrived at Mary's area, she advised me that the meeting was scheduled at 3:15 instead of 3:00 due to a vote on the Senate floor.

The agents peeled off at my office door and I entered the Oval Office to find a mound of paperwork that needed my signature. It was going to be a long day.

"Mary, see if Andy is back yet, and if he is, have him come in, please."

"He is back, sir, I'll let him know."

I finished signing the daily correspondence that the President sends out to various agencies, people, and for assorted causes, such as Special Olympics. This was an almost daily routine that would not vary much no matter where I would be.

Andy Carter came into the Oval Office and asked, "What's new, Mr. President?"

"Andy, we are sponsoring a peace conference in Jordan with the leaders of the Middle East. I am waiting to be connected with King Hussein to request that he host the summit. Syria is about to try nuclear blackmail against Israel and I'm sure you know how that would play out."

"Yes, the Middle East would be one giant ash tray."

"A couple of things I want you to put together. First, get a quick timetable together for the total withdrawal of all American land forces from Iraq and Afghanistan. George Bush's folly of a war is finally going to end along with the constant bloodletting of the national treasury. Second, put together an overview of any foreign aid to the Middle East, no matter the kind. I want to know what America spends each year on any country over there, including Israel. Finally, get together with Secretary Dukewell at State and have an agenda drawn up for the summit. We need to make a serious attempt at peace in the Middle East once and for all, and if that means taking something from Israel in order to achieve peace, then so be it."

"Let me remind you of the Israeli lobby, they will fight this with all their might."

"Fuck the Israeli lobby. I'm not the President of Israel, I'm the President of the United States and that is my responsibility."

The phone ringing interrupted our conversation.

"Yes?"

"Mr. President, King Hussein on line one."

"This is President Windsor, how are you, Your Majesty?"

"I am fine, Mr. President, and you?"

"I'm doing well, thank you. I have something rather serious to talk to you about."

"Yes, sir, go ahead."

"I'm hoping you and your kingdom would be willing to host a peace conference with the heads of state of the Middle East. There is an urgent need for this if we are to avoid a possible nuclear confrontation in your backyard. This would need to happen fairly quickly as the need is urgent."

"I am more than willing to play any part in a process that would lead this region towards peace and away from war. Who would be in attendance?"

"The heads of state for Syria, Egypt, Saudi Arabia, Iran, Israel, and the United States, and of course you. I can't stress enough the importance of this meeting."

"You yourself would be coming, Mr. President?"

"Yes. At the moment, nothing is more important than resolving the issues that have led to war after war in the Middle East. President Hassad is extending invitations, and we will talk to the Israelis."

"You have my complete cooperation, Mr. President. We can host the summit at Amman by the Dead Sea, a beautiful place that is conducive to the aims of the summit."

"Thank you, Your Majesty, our State Department will be in touch with your Foreign Ministry to work out all the details."

"Fine. I look forward to hosting this event."

The conversation ended, serious planning could now get underway.

"Andy, have State contact the other countries involved and get them on board. Let's get this summit underway within thirty days."

"Yes, Mr. President. You realize of course that Iran will be a very difficult part of this equation, right?"

"They meddle in everyone's affairs in the Middle East more than we do. They are essential to the process, unfortunately. How did your visit to the Hill go regarding Wilson's nomination?"

"No one expects that there will be any problems getting her confirmed. They are surprised that you chose a woman, though."

"Why? Isn't it about time a woman came into power in Washington in view of the mess that men have continued to make over the years this country has been in existence?"

"Well, actually, they felt that as a gay man, you would want a man in that office."

"Oh, for the love of God, the level of ignorance about human sexuality that these buffoons labor under knows no bounds! Well, fuck 'em, it's time they began to learn the truth about this issue."

"I must say also that they were shocked at your first legislative package. It wasn't at all what they were prepared for."

"Exactly as I told you, isn't it? We won't disappoint them in round two."

The rest of the day flew past as the business of state was systematically taken care of one issue at a time. The Congressional leaders were briefed on the Middle East summit and while they expressed total support for the concept, they felt I lacked experience to pull off anything meaningful. I urged them to submit any ideas that they had for consideration, and not to sell me short.

CHAPTER 9
TGIF

The week was coming to a tense close with all of the action in the Middle East. One good thing that occurred, of course, was the nomination of a new Vice-President. Confirmation hearings had already been scheduled for next Wednesday, and I hoped to have her sworn in by the following Friday.

"Mary, would you tell the appropriate people that I would like to spend my first weekend as President at Camp David? I want to leave this afternoon, and come back Monday morning."

"Of course, Mr. President."

It was already 1:30, and arrangements kicked into high gear. The professionals who moved the President were used to last minute arrangements being made, and a trip to Camp David involved only minimal assets. Shane opened the door and entered the office.

"Hi there," I said with a smile.

"Hello, Mr. President. We're going to Camp David?"

"Yes. I trust you'll be coming with me?"

"Of course, sir. Where you go, I go."

"I've never been to Camp David before. How close will your quarters be to mine?"

"About a hundred and twenty feet. There's a building that houses only Secret Service. There is also a small Marine detachment that patrols the perimeter and entry gates, plus the pilots of Marine One, and medical personnel."

"I guess I'm asking because I would enjoy your special company while up there; is that possible?"

"I'll make it possible, sir," Shane replied with a grin.

"Good. Then hopefully we can be together again tonight. I need you."

"And I you. I've always wanted to make love in the woods," he said with a laugh. "I'll let you know as soon as possible our departure time, but I would estimate you should prepare to leave in about an hour."

"Fine, Shane, thanks. Please let Mary know so that she can have James pack a bag for me for the weekend. You need to do the same, so why don't you take care of that?"

"Okay, I'll tend to that now. See you shortly."

I watched Shane walk out of the Oval Office and felt myself grow stiff in my pants. He was such a visual delight and the warmth in his voice made me grow more and more fond of this man. I took a few more phone calls, including one with the Secretary of State regarding the Middle East summit. I was assured that all arrangements would be swiftly made and dates set. The phone buzzed, bringing news I had been waiting to hear.

The one thing that I had in common with George Bush was that my canine companion was in fact a Scott Terrier, named Mary. She was a wonderful little Scottie with a personality that lit up the room when she entered. She was smart, a great hunter, and above all else, four legs of walking love. She was perhaps the only living thing that could bring a smile to my face quicker than Shane. Mary the Scottie had just arrived at the White House by special conveyance. She had been back in Pennsylvania at my home and had been kept there until I was settled into the White House. The door to my office flew open and in ran the true love of my life, visibly happy at seeing her daddy, jumping into my lap and washing my face with kisses. A low grrr sound emanated from her throat to let me know she was happy to see me. It was amazing how having her back with me brightened up my day and life. She truly was one of God's gifts to me.

"Mary, wanna go on a trip with daddy? Wanna go to the woods?"

Mary understood the word 'trip' and got even more excited, knowing we would be going somewhere together. She wagged her tail in anticipation; the tail that had been broken when she was only a couple days old by her canine father who clumsily stepped on her tail. Fortunately, you could not tell it was broken unless you felt her tail and found the telltale sign of a bump that indicated a break. I buzzed the human Mary and asked her to have canine Mary's things made ready to go to Camp David along with her.

Shortly after that call, Shane came into the office and announced that everything was ready and waiting on me as soon as Marine One landed on the White House lawn. A few moments later, I heard the sound of not one but three incoming helicopters and saw the green machines landing through my window. I got up and picked Mary up off the floor from where she was studying Shane and carried her with me as we left the office and headed out to the chopper. The front entrance ramp was down, and only I was permitted to use it under normal circumstances. Everyone else entered by the rear staircase.

I waved at the reporters and staff who were there to see me off and answered a couple of shouted questions about who I had in my arms. As I approached the staircase, the Marine on duty saluted, and I returned the salute and climb up the stairs into what was surprisingly a very comfortable helicopter. A second and third Marine helicopter with staff and additional Secret Service had taken off moments before from the same spot that Marine One now occupied. The Secret Service had requested that the Marines bring in three choppers so that no one would know which one I was on.

The engine started and we were off in a flash, slowly turning over Washington towards Maryland and Camp David, located in the mountains outside Emmitsburg. Mary insisted on looking out the window as I held her; her ears perked up as she tried to figure out how we were in the air. Behind me sat Shane and two other agents, along with Andy Carter who was coming for the weekend.

It was only a twenty-five minute flight to Camp David, and soon we were landing on the helipad at the Camp, which was covered with light snow. As soon as the rotor stopped turning and the front stairs were dropped, a Marine climbed out and stood at attention. I once again gathered up my canine companion and left by the front staircase, returning the salute I had received.

The air was crisp and clean-smelling with cloudy skies that held the promise of more snow. Colonel Manchuka, the Marine Commander of Camp David, was waiting my arrival. He snapped to attention, saluted and welcomed me to Camp David, the Presidential retreat.

"Thank you, Colonel, I'm pleased to make my first trip of what I assume will be many. I don't intend to spend many summer weekends in Washington."

"That's good to hear, sir; this place was built for the President's use and pleasure. There have also been historical meetings held here like the Camp David peace accords."

"Thank you again, Colonel, I appreciate your welcome."

"Yes, sir, if there is anything I can ever do, just ask me."

I was showed the way to the President's cabin, which was rustic in nature as all the buildings were. There was a fire in the fireplace, and comfortable furniture arranged inside. The bedroom held a queen size bed and the usual bedroom furniture with a private bathroom, and of course the ever present telephones. A second bedroom was directly next to the President's. Mary went exploring around the cabin in search of any stupid mice that might be present. If there were any around, there wouldn't be by the time Mary was done. Scott Terriers were originally bred for hunting vermin in the castles of Scotland, and the instinct was very strong in this Terrier.

I went back into the living room area to find Shane standing there.

"Shane, there are two bedrooms in this cabin, so take the other one, will you? No sense in making things more difficult by having you stay in the Secret Service cabin, agreed? Or do you feel that might make things a little obvious?"

"I didn't want to mention it, but the guys are already making fun of me for staying at the White House. So, staying here in this cabin will not make things any worse."

"What kinds of things are they saying?"

"What you would expect. That we're lovers, that I'm fucking the boss."

"Well, not yet you're not."

Shane smiled at that comment.

"Do you want to stay with your fellow agents, then? If you do, I won't be upset, I understand completely."

"Not on your life. They can say anything they want, the Director of the Secret Service fully supports my being close to you and he is the only one that can really fuck with my career. The others are just jealous."

"Fine, then it's settled. Put your gear in there and let's get comfortable."

As Shane unpacked, I changed out of my suit into jeans and a warm shirt. I was a bit troubled that the other agents were making fun of Shane, but I also knew Shane was a big boy and could take care of himself. Boy, was he a big boy! I made myself laugh out loud with that thought.

"What's so funny?"

"Oh nothing, Shane, just life, just life."

"Is there anything you'd like to do right now?"

"Hmm, yeah, but it can wait until tonight," I said with a smile.

"Yeah, I'm rather looking forward to that if I might say so."

"Until then, why don't we walk around this place and see what the layout is?"

"Okay, let's grab coats and go."

Upon leaving the Presidential cabin, I was met by my Marine Sergeant aide who asked if I needed anything. When I told him I wanted to look around, he offered to be my guide and I accepted. Camp David was a good deal bigger than I thought and as Mary ran through the brush hunting, I listened to the history of the various buildings, when they were built and who was President at the time. Presidential improvements were also pointed out to me, like the swimming pool put in for JFK to help him with his back. We paid a visit to the Marine barracks and when we entered someone yelled "Atten-hut!" and every guy in the barracks came to attention no matter where they were. I yelled, "As you were," and the various Marines relaxed and came up to me shaking my hand.

"You yelled out that command like you were a Marine, sir!"

"Not quite, Private, but I was an Air Force Officer."

Almost in unison, the assembled Marines expressed pride in their branch by moaning over the fact that I was prior Air Force.

"Okay, at ease, jarheads!" I said with a smile.

This order was met with a chorus of "Euu Rahs." I couldn't help but laugh out loud. This was a great bunch of kids who were as dedicated to their country as they were to the Corps. It was young men like these that I would have to send into war if that choice ever came to fall upon me. I wouldn't do it lightly. I made a quick inspection of their barracks, thanked them for their welcome and left. I left them all smiling, as they were proud to be connected with the Office of the President even in this small way.

"The pride of America right there, Shane."

"Yes, Mr. President, they surely are," came the reply.

"Sergeant, thank you for showing me around the buildings here, I appreciate it."

"Anytime, Mr. President," he said with a salute.

As we walked back towards the cabin, I said to Shane, "You know what I want scheduled? I want to visit and inspect a base from each of the armed forces, including the aircraft carrier Nimitz. I want to see what the living conditions and morale are like in the field."

"Yes, sir, and looking at all those fine boys in uniform wouldn't be bad either," Shane said with a grin.

"There is that, too, but that's just a side benefit. I believe our military has been misused in the past, and I want to know and understand the lives of the men and women that carry out the policy of the United States around the world, today, not from when I was in. I want to remember their faces if I ever have to decide whether to put them in harm's way."

Andy came up to us at that moment with a progress report on putting together the summit.

"Andy, I want you to schedule in the near future a tour of a military base from each of the Armed Services, to include a visit to the Nimitz in the Persian Gulf."

"Of course sir, but are you sure that the Nimitz is a good idea? You might be putting yourself in danger by being in the Gulf."

"Hell, Andy, they tried to kill me in the damn Capitol building, do you really think the Nimitz would be any more dangerous? I'd be dead if it wasn't for Shane here."

"Very well, sir, I'll put the inspections together. Now for the current mess in the Middle East – everyone has agreed to attend the summit but Saudi Arabia and Iran. The Saudis say that the problems between Syria and Israel do not affect them, and Iran just doesn't want to cooperate on anything with us."

"Call in the Saudi ambassador Monday morning. Get Prince Bandar Bin Sultan on the phone this afternoon before dinner. Prince Bandar spent years in Washington as the Saudi ambassador and knows us better than any other Saudi alive. He's now the Saudi Defense Minister, and next in line for the throne. Also, get me Secretary Andrews of the Energy Department on the phone today. As for Iran, I'll have to think about that, I'm open for suggestions on getting the Iranian president there."

"It will be tough, sir; they're in no mood to cooperate with us on anything. Look what you had to do just to get them to make their sub back off the Nimitz."

"We'll figure something out. Ask State to come up with suggestions also on this part of the problem."

We entered the cabin and Andy picked up a phone and requested that Prince Bandar of Saudi Arabia be contacted for me. After a wait of thirty minutes, the Prince was on the phone.

"Prince Bandar, President Windsor here."

"Good morning, Mr. President, or least it's morning here. What can I do for you?"

"Prince Bandar, you probably know that we want Saudi Arabia to be represented at a peace summit in Jordan to be held within the next couple of weeks in order to avoid a potential war that is looming over the Middle East. Your office has told my people that you are not willing to attend because it's not your problem. Is that correct?"

"Mr. President, we do not wish to get in the middle of problems that involve Israel. We see the situation as one concerning Syria and only Syria. We have no place there."

"So, if an agreement is reached that adversely affects your country, you don't care?"

"How could anything decided at such a conference affect the Kingdom?"

"How about a cloud of nuclear debris floating over your entire country, contaminating everything for a thousand or more years? No more oil revenue, no more holding up the rest of the world with oil economics? How's that affect you?"

"Very well, let me know when, and I'll be there. His Majesty is too ill to attend any conference anywhere that is not within the borders of the Kingdom."

"Please pass my best wishes for a speedy recovery on to His Majesty for me."

"I will indeed, Mr. President. Good bye."

"That takes care of Saudi Arabia. That leaves just the pain in the ass left. You work on that, Andy, talking once in a week to that jackass President is enough for me."

"Yes, sir, we're working on it now. The Secretary of Energy is on the phone for you, sir."

"President Windsor."

"Secretary Howell here, Mr. President."

"Margaret, I want you to move funding initiatives for alternative fuel sources to the top of your agenda. Now more than ever, we must eliminate the need for foreign oil. Come up with a dollar amount, no matter how large, to properly fund a joint project with private industry to come up with that source. I want substantial progress made within one year from today. The only other thing more important for you is the security of our nuclear facilities and the national secrets involving that technology. Plug the leaks that occurred under the previous administration at Livermore labs, again no matter the cost. Any questions?"

"No, Mr. President. I'll report to you on this at the next cabinet meeting."

"Fine, Margaret, see you then."

"Andy, join us for dinner?"

"Thank you, Mr. President, but I need to get back to Washington."

"Well, guess that's just the two of us then, Shane. Would you take care of ordering from the mess and have it sent over here?"

"You bet, am I off duty now?"

"You bet you are, Mister," I replied with a smile.

AFTER dinner and some television and the usual phone calls that came in until nine o'clock, things became quiet at Camp David. The only chore left was to walk Mary and then turn in for the night, a night that would not end when I turned in.

"Do you want me to go with you, sir?"

"No, Shane, you're off duty, remember? This place is crawling with Marines, I'll be just fine."

"Yeah, it's the Marines I'm worried about," Shane said with a laugh that cracked me up.

"Maybe I'll bring home a couple."

"Nah, I don't want to share you if that's okay with you."

I walked around for about twenty minutes because Mary was more interested in continuing the hunt than taking care of her business. Finally, she realized it was bedtime, and she took care of the necessary things and we went back to the cabin. After closing the door, Mary shook her body, which was the usual signal for, "I'm all done for the day, and can we go to bed now?"

"Not yet, Mary, you need to stay out here while Daddy takes care of someone special."

I looked around for Shane but could not find him in what in reality was a fairly small cabin considering its occupant. Finally I figured he went out to check in with the Service or something and went into my bedroom. There propped up on one arm was Shane, wearing nothing but a smile.

As I closed the bedroom door I said, "Damn, Shane, do you have any idea how sexy you look right now?"

"Why, Mr. President, I thought you said I always look sexy?"

"Yeah, but never more so than when you're naked."

I began to remove my clothes as Shane watched me take off each piece. By the time I was down to my Calvin's, I had a hard on that craved attention from the sexy man in my bed. I slipped off my shorts, freeing my cock for Shane's hungry gaze. He pulled back the covers and I got into bed with him. Our lips locked tightly as we embraced; our naked bodies clung to each other in such a way that I never wanted them parted. As we kissed, my hand went down his body rubbing his hard cock and balls. I wanted him badly and I knew what I needed.

I kicked the covers off, exposing our bodies to the firelight that came from the bedroom fireplace. I licked and sucked my way down Shane's body and when I reached his cock, I wasted no time; I took him in one swift action. Shane let out a little moan of pleasure as I began to slowly suck his beautiful dick while fondling his balls. His cock was smooth and hard and I paid the attention to it that it deserved. I could have spent all night between his legs, but I knew that would be hard to do without coming all over myself.

Shane pushed my head off his cock and pulled me up to his face where we kissed once more. He then flipped me over and began to run his tongue down my back, licking as he went. He did not stop when he reached my ass and in fact parted my ass cheeks and gave me that special pleasure that made fireworks go off in my head.

With an expert tongue, Shane worked my asshole over time and time again, setting all the nerve endings on fire with his skill. I found myself shoving my ass up into his probing tongue, wanting his entire head up my ass.

"Would you consider letting me fuck your gorgeous ass, David?"

This was what I wanted so rarely, but I wanted it with all my heart from this man. "Only if you promise to make it a good long fuck," I replied.

"I think I can manage that with great pleasure."

He drove his tongue back into my hole with even more eagerness this time. I felt myself open up like a lotus blossom waiting for the stem to be inserted. Shane got out of bed and went to the bag where he kept his nine-millimeter Glock in when he wasn't carrying it, and pulled out a tube of lube and several rubbers.

When I noticed the number of rubbers he had, I said, "Well, you certainly have confidence now, don't you?"

He laughed and said, "You never know how many of these things you're gonna need and I don't want to leave your bed again."

Before he could put one on, I began to suck his prick once again. I loved the feel and taste of his manhood and would have been happy if I was unable to possess any other man's dick the rest of my life.

He pulled out of my mouth and I felt like an infant whose mother had just pulled away her teat. Shane put on a rubber and a lot of lube while working a generous amount into my waiting hole. He spent a couple of minutes finger fucking me, making sure I was loose enough to take his nice sized cock.

"Are you ready?"

"I think I've been ready since I first laid eyes on you, stud, now take care of business."

Shane was a gentle lover; none of this 'climb on top and shove it in' stuff. He eased the head of his dick into my ass very slowly, whispering in my ear for me to relax. I was obviously not the first man that had been impaled on his manhood.

I felt him pop through the opening and now had the head of his dick in my ass. Despite the initial pain, I breathed deeply and forced myself to enjoy the fact that the man I was so attracted to was fucking me. I urged him on. He slowly began to insert the rest of his cock into my ass until I felt him sigh from pleasure at having his entire dick in my ass. Shane lay down on my back and whispered into my ear that he was in and for me to let him know when it was all right for him to fuck me.

"I'm fine, take me."

Permission granted, Shane began a slow withdrawal and reinsertion. He used long strokes instead of short fast ones. I was in heaven at the total pleasure of Shane fucking me, moaning from the joy of his attentions. He pulled out and told me to turn over which I willingly did. As he looked down into my eyes, he simply said, "I'm gonna fuck you good like you deserve."

I almost came just hearing that phrase. Shane lifted my legs up and pushed them back towards my head as he inched up on the bed. He quickly added more lube to his cock, and reinserted his prick deep into my waiting ass. Without question, Shane was managing to hit my prostate each time he thrust inwards. If asked to describe the feelings that I was experiencing, I would have been unable to do so. Shane picked up speed and began to really put it to me as I looked up into his eyes and saw the passion contained within them. I knew without doubt that Shane was fucking David Windsor and not the President. He bent his head and kissed me as he continued to drive his cock into me. He broke the kiss and threw his head back in pure pleasure, moaning as he continued his gentle yet firm assault on my ass.

I was surprised at how much I loved being dominated by Shane, as I was always the one who was on the top with other men in the past. I had determined before with others that I did not like being the 'catcher' but rather preferred the role of 'pitcher'. Maybe this time the difference was that this man had saved my life and that put me in a different frame of mind.

"Are you doing all right?"

"Fuck, yes," I replied with a smile and a groan.

He picked up his speed again, pounding into me until I was begging for more. I truly felt in perfect harmony with the ass fucking I was getting. After another couple of minutes of this more intense fucking, Shane pulled out, and told me to get up on my knees at the edge of the bed. I did as I was told once again.

Shane applied more lube to my now slightly sore asshole and standing, moved up to my ass where he inserted his cock once again. Now he began to fuck me while he stood next to the bed with my ass up in the air directly in front of his cock. He took no prisoners and his cock turned into a piston as he fucked me at full force and speed. I was learning what it truly meant to be soundly fucked by a man who knew what he was doing. I willingly gave Shane my ass for whatever abuse he deemed fit to hand out and continued to enjoy both the fuck and the feeling of being on the bottom and giving up control to the powerful man who was taking his pleasure the way he wanted.

After a slow moan in which I had assumed Shane was getting ready to blow his load, he pulled out, and I heard him rip off the rubber and felt his cock lay on top of my lower back just above my ass as stream after stream of hot come splashed all over my back. Shane continued to come for about half a minute before collapsing onto my back, immersing himself in his own fluids that pooled all over my skin. His breathing was very heavy and he pushed both arms under my chest and held me tightly to him. We lay there several moments like that until he got up, going into the bathroom to retrieve a towel that had the Presidential seal on it.

"No, get a wash cloth. I can't have the steward finding a come-stained towel in my bathroom," I said, laughing. Shane did as I suggested and came back with a wet warm washcloth and wiped off my entire back, asshole, and then himself.

"Now for you, what would please you most?"

"What would please me most, I shall deny myself for the time being. I intend to fuck you as silly as you've just done to me. But I want you horny when I put it to you. For now, just suck me off if you would be so kind."

"With pleasure."

Instead of just going down between my legs and swallowing my cock, Shane lay on his back and pulled me up to his face. He opened his mouth and said, "If you don't want to fuck ass right now, then fuck my face, and shoot your load down my throat."

"That's not necessary, Shane. I can just give you a pearl necklace," I answered with a smile.

"No, I want your load. It's what I want after your taking the fucking I just gave you."

"No further argument from me then," I said as I put my dick into Shane's waiting mouth and began to fuck his face.

I found that Shane could take all of me down his throat without gagging which gave me a very pleasurable blowjob. I was so keyed up from the butt fucking Shane had given me that it only took about two minutes before I felt my load begin to blow. As the first stream of come flowed out of my cock, I shoved down Shane's throat and timed my thrusts so that each major stream went in the same way. When my climax ebbed, I began to come in Shane's mouth so that he got the full flavor of my spunk. Shane eagerly swallowed and sucked hard on my cock, making sure that he got every drop that my balls had to offer. Finally, when my prick started to go limp, he let go and it fell out of his mouth and onto his chin, where he swiped it one final time with his tongue.

I collapsed onto the bed fully exhausted with a very satisfied libido and a sore asshole. Shane was a very good cocksman, but he left me knowing that I had been well fucked. As my own cock now relaxed into full flaccid state, Shane snuggled up against me and thanked me for a good fuck.

"That was an outstanding fuck, thank you. I got the feeling that you were a virgin, am I correct?"

"Actually, you are correct. I've allowed other men to attempt to have my ass, but none of them knew what the hell they were doing. I remember one Marine in particular who begged to fuck me and when I said yes, he hit my ass like he was taking a beachhead. I terminated the operation. You, on the other hand, knew exactly what you were doing, and brought me great pleasure. Have you fucked many men?"

"I've been fucking boys and men since I was sixteen, and the neighborhood boys my age wanted to both suck me off and bend over for me. So, yes, I have a fair amount of experience at taking a guy's ass. But none have been as pleasurable as having yours."

I looked at Shane and said, "Bullshit!" and laughed out loud. "If you've done that much butt pirating, then I know you've had better and more experienced men than me, now cut the shit."

Shane laughed in return. "There have been more experienced men who could take a pounding right off, but there is something special when you know you're fucking a virgin. I knew you had no experience, which is why I took so much time eating you out first. That's the best way to loosen up a man to take your rod."

"You did an outstanding job and for the first time, I was fully fucked and loved every minute of it, even if I am a little sore around the hole at the moment."

"That will pass in a few hours and all you'll be left with is the pleasant memories of taking a man in the time honored way. Now, I suppose I should go to my bed and let you get to sleep."

"No, Shane, stay with me. You're the first man to fuck me and I think it only appropriate that you now sleep with me. What do you say? Do you want to sleep with the President of the United States?"

Shane's response was to get out of bed, brush his teeth and let a very happy Mary into the room. She bounded onto the bed and curled up over the top of my head on the pillow. Shane threw another log on the fire and moved his bag that held his service weapon next to the bed, sliding back in beside me and pulling the sheets up. His last move was to roll over on his side towards me and put his arm around me. He kissed me on the chest and the lips and put his head down on my chest and said good night.

I felt incredible. I had just ended one of the finest sexual experiences of my life, and now got to sleep with a man that I was fond of ... or was I falling in love with this man? Boy, would that complicate things – falling in love with my bodyguard. But then again, what was simple about anything in my life?

I woke up to the sound of a bugle playing the Star Spangled Banner, which meant that it was 8 o'clock. I turned my head to see if Shane was awake and found that he had already left my bed and gone about his duties. I don't know why I had expected him to be on some kind of vacation here at Camp David, but he was still with the Secret Service and was in fact now on duty.

I got out of bed and quickly showered off the remaining evidence of last night's love making session. My asshole was still sore, but not as bad as it was right after Shane had finished. He was right, the discomfort would quickly fade.

As I stepped out of the shower, a Marine orderly was standing there with a towel. He scared the shit out of me since I wasn't expecting anyone to be there, let alone when I was nude. He was a good looking Marine around twenty-four and simply said, "Your towel, sir." His eyes never dropped below my own.

I took the towel and thanked him. "What's your name, Marine?"

"PFC Callaghan, sir. I'm your valet while here at Camp David."

"What is your first name, Marine? If a man is going to be standing there in the morning seeing me nude, I should at least know his first name, don't you think?"

"Yes, sir, I suppose you're right, sir," he said, smiling. "My name is Jack."

"Well, Jack, thank you for the towel. What else do you do around here?"

"Basically sir, I perform the same duties as your White House Valet."

"Very well, but please don't enter the bedroom area until you hear the water running."

"Yes, sir, your Secret Service agent already informed me of that, sir."

"Oh, he did, okay then. Have you laid out clothes for this morning?"

"Yes, sir, I checked your agenda and didn't find any meetings scheduled, so I laid out casual clothes to include jeans. Is that acceptable, sir?"

"Totally, Jack, thank you. That will be all."

"Yes, sir, I just have to clean up your bathroom when you're finished and change your towels. When you go to breakfast, I will make up your bedroom, sir. May I say something, sir?"

"Of course, Jack."

"Please forgive me, Mr. President, if I overstep myself here, but I wish to tell you that since you are my first Commander in Chief who is gay like me, that you can be assured of total discretion on my part about anything I might see or encounter. You have my word of honor as a Marine on that, sir."

"Thank you, Jack. That's rather bold of you to come out to me, isn't it?"

"Sir, since I voted for you, I followed all of your campaign speeches and I know that one of the things you wish to do is get rid of 'don't ask, don't tell' and allow us gay service members to serve openly. So, yes sir, I'm taking a risk, but I also trust you."

"Thank you, Jack, you can. Now I need to get dressed and head to breakfast."

"Do you want breakfast served here in the cabin, Mr. President?"

"What are my options?"

"Well, sir, they're a little limited. You can eat here, or the mess hall reserved for guests of the President and aides, or with the Marine guard in the military mess hall."

"Who has the worst food?"

"Well, the food is generally very good since this is Camp David, but I would have to say that the food we Marines eat is probably of a slightly lesser caliber than the other options."

"Well, that settles it then, it's the Marine chow hall."

As I exited the cabin after dressing I ran into two Marine guards and Shane. The Marines snapped to attention and saluted, and Shane smiled and asked me if I was headed towards the VIP Mess.

"No, I want to see how the food is that the Marines here eat."

"It's your stomach, sir."

"Before we enter the mess hall, I need to tell you something important," Shane whispered, his voice full of concern.

"What is it?"

"When I woke up this morning before you, I was getting out of bed, naked of course, when a young Marine with a blond crew cut opened the door to your bedroom and caught me as I was. He blushed and whispered his apologies, but he was looking at my dick when he closed the door.

"Was it Jack, my Marine valet?"

"Yes, sir. I'm not sure how much fuss this is going to create."

"It's all right, it's not going to cause any fuss. Now I understand why he said what he did to me. I got out of the shower and found this Marine waiting with a towel for me. Once I got over the shock that it was someone other than you, he introduced himself, and said that I could count on his total discretion, and then came out to me as being gay. It made no sense then for his doing that, but it does now. So, I wouldn't worry about it at all. I'll have another talk with him."

"Okay, that's a load off my mind. Felt like shooting the cute little bugger."

"Glad you didn't, that would have been such a terrible waste of young manhood."

As we entered the Marine Mess, once again I heard the order, "Atten-hut!" and responded once again, "As you were."

"Good morning, Mr. President. Your mess hall is across the way sir, this is Marine food here."

"That, Captain, is why I chose to eat here. I want to see what your food is like over here."

"As you wish, sir, this way please."

We walked over to the chow line that had only two Marines in it at the time. I took a tray and walked down the line. The cooks looked quite flustered that they were serving their Commander in Chief. I took some scrambled eggs, bacon, toast, coffee and orange juice and walked over to a table that had three other Marines sitting there.

"Mind if I join you, gentlemen?" I asked.

"No sir," came back the answer in unison. I began to eat the eggs and immediately noticed that they seemed to have less taste than normal. The coffee was weak but everything else was fine.

"What's with the eggs, guys? They taste a little off."

They all smiled at me and one answered, "Why sir, they're powdered eggs, that's why. Only the best for the Marines!" They all chuckled.

Shane just stood silently over in a corner watching us. I looked at him once and smiled, briefly remembering the night before. There was no response from Shane to my smile.

As I finished my breakfast and chat with the Marines, I got up and took my tray over to the kitchen for cleaning. I turned around to one of the line cooks and asked, "Who's the ranking Marine present now?"

"Why, that would be Major Daniels who is eating in the back, sir."

"Tell him I would like to see him, please."

"Yes, Mr. President, right away."

A tough old leatherneck of a Marine Major appeared within moments, snapped to attention and said, "Major Daniels reporting as ordered, sir."

"At ease, Major. Look, I understand through taste and conversation that the Marines are fed powdered eggs, is that correct, Major?"

"Yes sir, that is correct. Whole eggs are saved for the VIP's that visit, as well as you of course, sir."

"Major, from now on, I want the very same food that is served to me to be available to all Marines and other military personnel who work this post, is that clear? I know some hardships are necessary for military personnel to endure; it's the nature of the beast. But we are not in a war zone, and there is no reason in my book that the men can't eat well."

"Yes, sir, I understand and will make the commanding officer aware of your orders."

"Very well, Major, and that is effective no later than tomorrow morning."

"Yes, sir."

I left the Marine mess hall with Shane and headed back to the cabin where I found Mary wanting to go for a walk. Putting her leash on, we took her out into the woods. Once I remembered that we were in a fenced in compound, I took Mary off her leash and let her run free. She loved it and immediately started her hunting routine. I laughed as she dove into the underbrush trying to scare the prey out into the open, and sticking her nose down into any hole she could find, without much success. After a time, we went back to my cabin and settled in for the rest of the morning. Everything appeared to be quiet for the moment on the world stage and there were no urgent phone calls to return.

Late that afternoon, Andy Carter called to confirm that they had convinced Iran to attend the peace summit and that the date was set for February 2nd, in Amman, Jordan. Arrangements now went into full swing for planning the agenda as well as the logistics.

"Andy, break up the return trip with a two day state visit to England. Let Buckingham Palace know the dates and see if that would work for them. More than likely we will stay at the Palace with my cousin, the King."

Hanging up the phone, I turned to Shane. "You better let your bosses know that we have a Middle East trip coming up along with a stopover in Great Britain on the return. Have them coordinate with Andy."

"Yes, Mr. President. I can tell you this, they won't be too happy. We're going to be going into a region of the world where we are already hated, and then on top of that, the American president is a homosexual. You're going to have a large security detail."

"Will you be with me?"

"Of course, Mr. President, I will be as close to you as your Calvin's," he said with an evil grin. I laughed in response and replied, "I'll count on that, Agent Thompson."

Day passed into evening, and the fireplaces were once again stoked in order for them to put out maximum heat and light. Jack, my valet, lit the one in the bedroom about seven o'clock.

I took this opportunity to have another chat with Jack.

"Jack, I'd like a word with you."

"Yes, Mr. President, did I do something wrong?"

"In talking with a certain agent of the Secret Service, I understand that you entered my bedroom this morning and might have seen something unexpected. Is that what made you come out to me?"

"Yes, sir, I figured Agent Thompson would tell you that I saw him getting out of your bed naked, and that you might be concerned about the word getting around that you were sleeping with your agent. I wanted you to know that would never happen and why it would never happen. The best way to do that was to tell you the fact that I'm also gay. I hope you're not upset and believe you can trust me."

"Yes, Marine, I believe that you would keep your word to your Commander in Chief. I also value loyalty and hard work. Do you like your assignment here, Jack?"

"Camp David? Yes, sir. It's an honor for any Marine to be assigned to duties that involve you. Sure it gets lonely here, but it's still Camp David."

"How would you like to work for me full time?"

"I'm not sure what you mean, sir?"

"I mean how would you like to be transferred to the White House as a Marine enlisted aide to me?"

"Oh my God, sir! Are you serious? There's nothing better than being assigned to the White House and to serve you fulltime sir would be incredible! So, yes sir, I would like that. But please, sir, you don't have to do this for me to keep quiet."

"I know that, Jack, or you would be guarding a pigpen on Guam. I'll make the arrangements to have your transferred as soon as possible. Loyalty has its rewards, Marine."

"Yes sir, thank you, sir!"

Shane was smiling broadly when I left the bedroom as he had overheard every word that was said. It was his job to stay close to me, and he took that job seriously.

"So, do I have to be concerned about potential competition from a young Marine stud?"

"Shane, you dick, it's bad enough my Secret Service Agent is fucking me without involving a Marine also. No, military men are off limits due to the chain of command. As much as I wouldn't mind putting it to him, it isn't possible."

"Better not, or you'll be known as the gay Bill Clinton," he said with a loud laugh.

"Look, with all that's beginning to happen with the Middle East Summit, we better head back to D.C. tomorrow instead of Monday morning. Let everyone know, will you?"

"Yes sir, will do. Does that mean we might have one more night together?"

"I don't see why not. Besides, it's your turn in the barrel, stud."

"With pleasure, boss," Shane said with that certain grin that looks so evil.

AFTER we had a great dinner and I took Mary on a long walk around the compound, I returned to the cabin to find Shane sitting in front of the living room fireplace with two drinks before each of our places.

"I thought you might like a drink as it's a bit cold outside."

"Are we alone?"

"Yes, not even Jack is here. I think he's off duty and another Marine is on duty in his place."

"Let's not have to break in another Marine tonight, huh?"

"No, sir. Let's watch a movie and go to bed, what do you say?"

"Kind of eager to get to bed, aren't you?"

"You bet, I want to see what you can do with that weapon in your pants. Been wanting it all day long."

"Not a problem, stud."

"Mountain air makes me horny."

"Guess we will have to spend a lot of time here at Camp David, then."

A few phone calls came in, nothing important. We were about ready to head into the bedroom when I got a call from the main gate that the Director of the CIA was waiting to see me. I told the gate to let him in and for him to come directly to my cabin.

"Shane, the Director of the CIA is on his way here. Must be important or he wouldn't have traveled here to see me when we are coming back to D.C. in the morning."

"When he gets here, I'll be back in the kitchen area making us a drink for the bedroom. Holler if you need me."

Before I could answer, a knock on the door announced the arrival of the CIA Director. I let him in and told him to take off his coat and sit down by the fire. Mary made her usual cursory examination of the visitor, found nothing to object to, and curled up at my feet.

"Okay, shoot, what has brought you all the way up here on a Saturday night?"

"Mr. President, the Agency has come into possession of information that your trip to Jordan has already leaked all over the Middle East and that a certain group of terrorists are planning on an attempt to assassinate you while you are there. We find the information credible."

"Agent Thompson, would you come in here, please?"

Shane came into the room and I briefly explained what had been told to me so far.

"Do we know which group it is?" asked Shane.

"Yes, we have a clear idea. It appears that Muqtada al-Sadr and his al-Mahdi militia are behind the move, with assistance being supplied by Bin Laden's people. They see this as a way to pay America back in one blow for the invasion of Iraq. So what we have here is two agendas. One, the Syrians and their bomb, and now the radicals and their plot to kill you. The CIA officially advises you, Mr. President, to cancel your participation in the summit. Send the Vice-President, who should be confirmed by then."

"No, I can't do that. I have demanded that the heads of state themselves be in attendance. How can I turn around and send my number two? ,We would be the laughing stock of the world, and we have enough of a job rebuilding our credibility as it is. Shane, the Secret Service is going to have to step it up on this trip. You better put in a call to your Director and give him as much advance notice as we can."

"Yes, sir, I'll do that now," Shane said as he left the room to use the phone in his own bedroom.

"Al, is there any way to take out the principal planners before I arrive in the Middle East as a way to short circuit the plot?"

"More than likely, Mr. President, but that's going to create a firestorm that will more than likely blow back on our troops in Iraq. Up until this point, the Militia has been more or less quiet when it came to our forces for the last six months; that will change. But if those are your orders, the CIA can do it."

"Do we have him under surveillance?"

"Yes, sir, as best we can. I could probably guarantee you that if we don't know exactly where he's at one point in time; we would in a matter of three hours."

"Okay, for now, continue the surveillance. We strike if we have no other choice or if he gets more ambitious than he is now. Any indications at all that Iran is part of this plot?"

"No, sir, and the Iranians know that if they were caught in a plot like this, they would open themselves up for a nuke attack from our forces. They back Hezbollah as you know, and you're not a target for them."

"Okay, I want to know the second you do should any country that is part of this summit become involved somehow in this plot. Can you move more human assets into the Amman, Jordan area where the summit will be held?"

"Yes, sir, we have a few people on the payroll there. I'll move them immediately."

As the CIA director left the cabin, I realized just how vulnerable I would be in Jordan. I would have to rely on the Secret Service heavily and follow their advice if I wanted to stay alive. Shane came back into the living room and told me he had gotten through to the Director who also wanted me to cancel the trip.

"You told him that wasn't going to happen, right?"

"Of course. As soon as we land back in D.C., the Director has called a special meeting of the entire protection management team. It looks like as many as one hundred agents will be traveling with you to this summit."

"If that's what it takes, then that's what we'll have to do. Look, stud, this whole thing has put me off of my game; do you mind if we just sleep tonight?"

"Of course not. I'm a little worried myself. But as soon as we get a handle on things, I intend to get your handle on me," he said with a laugh.

"Thanks to Harry Truman, you can visit any time we like, and I imagine that will be in the next couple of days, Shane. Let's go to bed, huh?"

"Sounds fine to me. I'll turn off the lights and let the control center know you're in bed, and I'm off duty. Be in shortly."

CHAPTER 10
MADAM
VICE-PRESIDENT

We landed on the White House lawn at 10:57 A.M. Sunday morning. Mary and I left Marine One by the front door and everyone else by the rear stairs. A small group of office staff were there to greet me and ask me how I liked the Camp. I chatted with one of my press people as Mary watered the lawn and ran to catch up to me. Once inside, I headed directly to the Oval Office to see if there was anything further on the Middle East threat.

The peace summit was now just fourteen days away, and a lot of work had to be done before I left American soil. For one thing, the new Vice-President had to be in place. After I sat down, I asked Mary my secretary to get the leaders of the Hill on the phone. Even though it was Sunday morning, anyone could be reached by the White House if necessary.

When the Congressional leadership was tied in on a secure conference line, I laid it out for them.

"Gentlemen, a matter has come up that makes it imperative that Governor Wilson's nomination as Vice-President be swiftly moved through the process and finished this week, preferably by Thursday. Can this be done?"

"Mr. President, that gives us almost no time for questions, but merely to, in effect, rubber-stamp your choice. What could be so important as to make you request this?"

"Senator, there is a plot to kill me shortly after I step off Air Force One in Jordan. The al-Sadr Militia is behind it with help from our Bin Laden friends. I must have a fully briefed and settled-in Vice-President before taking off on this trip. She must have time to be briefed on the million things a Vice-President must know. If I wasn't convinced of the seriousness of this situation, I would not be asking you to speed this up beyond normal protocol."

"Certainly something can be done about this to prevent any chance that you might be assassinated, can't it?"

"The CIA and other intelligence organs of the U.S. are working on it, but I do not want a Constitutional crisis should I be killed. Look, Wilson is clean, wholesome, intelligent, and will be good for women and for the country. Let's get this done quickly."

"Very well, Mr. President. I'll begin the hearings on Tuesday instead of Wednesday, and have a vote of the full Senate by Wednesday evening. Will that do?"

"Senator, that would be outstanding. It is for the good of the nation, after all."

"Very well, Mr. President. But to return the favor, I would like an invitation to the state dinner when your cousin pays us a visit!"

I laughed out loud at the request and said, "I think we can arrange that, Senator. Good day, sir."

I picked up the phone and called Andy Carter to give him the news, and then informed Governor Wilson of the new schedule and requested that she and her son move to Washington no later than the next day. I wanted her here in D.C. when the hearings started. I asked Andy to make sure that the Naval Observatory was ready to receive its next tenant.

Next I called in my military aide de camp, Colonel Baxter, and requested that he contact Military Personnel to have the Marine Sergeant from Camp David transferred to the White House to act as my enlisted aide de camp. It would be nice to have that young man around. He was smart, gay, and loyal and would go out of his way to assist me in matters that pertained to military and other duties. Colonel Baxter informed me that he would be on duty in the White House within forty-eight hours.

I was finished for the day as it was Sunday, and Shane, little Mary and I headed upstairs to the residence. I got out of my clothes and into a pair of gym shorts and a t-shirt. I wanted to be comfortable and there was no reason I couldn't. Shane dressed down as well, but nowhere near as 'down' as I. Henry came in and asked if I would be dining by myself or with Agent Thompson, to which I replied, "Two for dinner, Henry." I wondered to myself if Henry ever took a day off. Later I found out that if I was out of town, he was off. If I was in town, he was on duty. I thought that was a bit much for a man of his years. Henry had been in White House service for forty-three years, and although he could retire any time he wanted, the White House and its temporary residents were his life.

Shane and I spent the rest of the afternoon watching movies in the White House theater which carried the latest Hollywood releases. After all, it wasn't like I could just jump into the car and go to the local cinema. We ate at six o'clock, watched the news, had a couple of drinks and went to bed around nine. It was a peaceful, relaxing afternoon and evening.

The night duty agent was patrolling the hallway as usual. I buzzed Shane's room and when he answered, I whispered, "Feel like walking through dusty cobwebbed passages and out through a bookcase?"

Shane chuckled. "I'll be right over."

The bookcase creaked a little and swung open, revealing Shane standing there in the entranceway in all his glory, wearing only socks and a jock strap. I laughed out loud seeing him like that. He managed to take my breath away with his pure male beauty while at the same time cracking me up, especially since he had a massive cobweb on his head. He closed the bookcase, brushed off his head and chest and came over to the bed where he landed a kiss right on my mouth. As he kissed me, I reached up and fondled his jock pouch which made him hard almost at once.

We fell back together onto the bed where we continued to kiss long and deep. I began to realize that I was developing feelings for this man; he had become more to me than just a fuck with a hot guy.

He finally came up for air, and started to remove what little clothing I had on. I did not resist one bit as I enjoyed his taking command of the situation even though he was going to be on the bottom tonight. Finally, I was naked and I pushed Shane onto his back where I pulled off his jock, freeing his beautiful cock. His sheer manliness made my heart beat faster just seeing him. I leaned over his body and said, "Tonight, you're the one taking directions, Mister."

Shane smiled and said, "Anything you want, anything."

I began to cover his face, neck and chest with kisses and then dragged my hot tongue down his body towards the prize that I so often thought about. He was already hard and waiting for attention with anticipation. As I ran my tongue down the underside of his shaft, he writhed in delight at the contact. I got to his balls where I slowly licked each one, taking it in my mouth and gently sucking on it. I heard a soft moan escape his lips and knew that I was giving him what he wanted.

I let his balls fall from my mouth and mounted his chest so that my cock was pointing directly at his full wet lips. I smiled down at him and said, "Open up, honey, Daddy has a great big surprise for you." I slipped my cock into Shane's mouth and he sucked at it hungrily. I took his head in my hands and began to slowly face fuck him, being gentle and careful not to force my dick down his throat. He worked my cock with his tongue as I slid in and out of his mouth, each time inserting just a little bit more until finally my balls were resting on his chin. His oral skills were highly evolved and I felt myself enjoying the sucking a little too much and withdrew my cock from his face.

"Oh, not yet," Shane said with lust in his voice.

"No, I have other plans for you tonight and it does not include popping off after two minutes."

I went back down Shane's chest and stomach and took his dick into my mouth, slowly working it like I knew he liked it. I had to fight the urge to make him come then and there, but that would have denied me my first experience topping this beauty of a man. It was obvious that we were both super horny as we were dripping with urgency, both of us panting in quick short breaths.

"Dave, take what you've been waiting for, just be a little slow since it's been four years since I had anyone up my ass, and it was only one time."

"Well, hell, don't you know the gay rule about ass love? If you've only been had once, and it's been more than a year, you are officially a virgin once again. It just grows back magically. So I need to take care of that, because there are never virgins sleeping in the White House."

Shane's response was to simply roll over and shift his legs to the side slightly, which made the muscles in his ass dance. I fell on each cheek and bathed them with my tongue, finishing by running my tongue down the crack of his just washed ass. I could smell the soap on his flesh and knew he'd been counting on this happening.

I spread his ass cheeks and blew across his entranceway, which sent a chill up his back, goose bumps rising along his spine. I devoured his love tunnel with as much gusto as I could. If it had been that long and only once since he had been fucked, he was going to be tight, and probably tense. It was my job to put him at ease so that both of us enjoyed this particular act of love making. When I was finished, I leaned over to the nightstand and withdrew a box. Inside the box were a rubber and a small tube of lube.

"Come on, stud, take it. I need you inside of me now!"

"Shhh," I said, putting my finger up to my mouth. "The agent is going to hear you and then he'll be at the keyhole listening to every thrust and moan."

"Pure jealousy is all that it would be," he replied laughing.

I put a generous amount of lube on my finger and worked it into Shane's willing ass and then put the rubber on. I decided to take him on his back so that I, like him, could look into his eyes as I fucked him silly.

"Roll over, stud, your legs are going into the air."

I lubed up my cock and pressed the head of my dick against Shane's asshole, finding it easier to penetrate him than I thought it was going to be. I let his ass adjust to my dick, and then slowly eased the rest of it in. His ass felt hot and ready, and I began a slow fucking motion. Shane's head went back as he stifled a moan from deep within. Both of his nipples were erect, telling me he was fully aroused and enjoying the fucking he was beginning to get. His cock bounced around while touching his navel, hard as rock.

"Give it to me, David, give it to me hard!"

I complied with his request and began to slam into him hard. Each time I thrust all the way in, the contact between our bodies made a sound. My balls bounced off his ass each time I entered him. At his urging, I withdrew all the way out, and then slammed all the way in to the base of my cock. Shane thrashed around on the bed, obviously enjoying the banging I was giving him. I felt my climax begin to build so I slowed down to prevent an early climax, only to be told in no uncertain terms by my bedmate to keep fucking him like he was a cheap nickel-dime New Orleans whore.

In another minute of intense fucking, I began to come. I grunted each time a spurt left my dick and filled the rubber that was soundly encasing my cock. As I was coming, Shane was jacking his own cock until, as I reached the end of my climax, Shane began to spurt all over his stomach and chest. It truly was a great sex session even though it lasted far shorter than I had planned. I fell down upon Shane's chest and let his legs down along side me at the same time. His juices now covered my own chest as I lay on top of him breathing heavily. We both smiled and he kissed me deeply once again.

"That was a great fuck, David, I loved it. Thank you."

"Believe me; you have one fine ass that takes a cock like a duck takes to water. I came so hard, my balls hurt!"

After another minute or so I got up and went to my bathroom and retrieved a washcloth to wipe us off. When I had reasonably cleaned us both up, I fell down next to Shane again. I just wanted to rest my head on his chest and run my hand through his pubic hair.

"I wish you were not the President."

His comment shocked me. "Why, Shane?"

"Because maybe then we could plan some sort of life together. I think I have feelings for you."

"And I for you," I admitted. "But I don't see why my being President should preclude any sort of emotional investment in each other. After all, we have the perfect reason to be together all the time, and having sex is obviously no problem."

"Yes, but for the most part, I have to leave your bed each night. That I don't like."

"Well, yes, that you must do. Let me think on it and see what I can come up with. But at least you can stay here with me for another hour or so; as long as we make sure we don't fall asleep and get found by James or Henry in the morning. They would die of a heart attack, I'm afraid."

"I'm really tired after that tremendous fucking you just gave me and to be safe, I'd better go now so that doesn't happen. Do you mind?" he asked tentatively

"Of course not."

"Besides, I know I'm going to be in a lot of meetings tomorrow due to your trip to the Middle East and the threat against your life. So, I'd better be well rested."

He kissed me tenderly and left my bed the way he entered; only this time, he carried the jockstrap. I pulled the covers up over me and dreamed of having Shane as a lover. Could it be?

My canine companion seemed able to sense that I was both happy and sad at the same time, and Mary snuggled up against my head on the pillow. I ran my hand over her coat a couple of times, and drifted off to sleep.

James woke me the next morning by knocking on the door and entering.

"Good morning, Mr. President, I hope you slept well?"

I yawned and stretched and replied, "Actually I had a great night's sleep, but it's back to the official grind now, isn't it?"

"Yes, I'm afraid it is, Mr. President."

While I got showered and dressed, James had Mary walked and she was waiting for me when I came out of the bathroom, having combed my hair for the final time. As I left my bedroom and went to the dining room, Mary followed, trying to get more attention from me. When I sat down at the table, her attention switched quickly to wondering if she would get anything to eat, rather than just wanting to be petted on the head.

As usual, Shane had already eaten and was on duty in the residence. I quickly ate some eggs and bacon, orange juice and coffee, and headed to the Oval Office. As I finished, Henry set a small plate down on the floor with two eggs, scrambled, just for Mary, making a new friend for life.

Shane looked stunning as usual in his dark suit and led the way to the elevator with a second agent behind me.

I said good morning to everyone and entered the office. Mary the dog took her usual place on the floor behind me and to the right of the flag. Mary the secretary informed me that Governor Wilson would be in Washington no later than 6:00 this evening and would be taken directly to the Naval Observatory which would be her new residence. A knock on my door announced that it was time for my morning briefing from the CIA and other agencies dedicated to intelligence.

"Good morning, Mr. President."

"Good morning, and how is the CIA today?"

"Well, sir, we have more news that is troubling. In attempting to discern who exactly was behind the plot to kill you in the Middle East, we have come up with a connection to Saudi Arabia. It would appear that the Saudis are financing the operation against you in an attempt to maintain peace in their kingdom. We have come across a written agreement between the Saudis and the terrorists that states quite plainly that in exchange for seven million dollars to finance their operation against you, they will ensure peace in Saudi Arabia for the next year or more."

"Do we have a copy of this agreement? Who signed on behalf of the Saudis, surely not the King?"

"Yes, sir, we have a copy of the agreement and the details about when it was signed and who was there. As for the Saudi signature, it was Bandar."

"So, they're using our own oil money against us, and the man who was Washington's ambassador from Saudi Arabia for so long and understands us the best is the Judas in all of this. Director, verify all of this from an independent source if you can, and let me know."

"That might be difficult but we'll give it a try. Now, as for the plot itself; from what we have been able to learn, there will be a two pronged attack. The first part involves the use of a sniper in an attempt to take you out at a public appearance. The second will be with a bomb or shoulder launch rocket which will try and take out Air Force One. Since getting a bomb on board Air Force One would be next to impossible, we're gearing up for anti-missile defense. Unfortunately, we've lost contact with this source and have been unable to refine the details any further."

"I want all intelligence agencies to focus on Saudi Arabia in order to determine the exact extent of their activities designed to harm me or America. I haven't trusted them since the attacks on the World Trade Center and the Pentagon. The last public thing I heard about them is that they were trying to buy contracts to control our ports."

"All right, sir, I'll get that out this morning. Elsewhere, the Chinese are cracking down on protestors using the Army and are reportedly shooting people in the streets. Of particular interest to them once again are the students, who have been protesting the lack of personal freedoms and censorship of the internet. As usual, the Party is controlling all responses to the protest and is dictating how the army should react."

"Okay, keep me posted on any increase in violence. Sounds like our Secretary of State should be involved deeply with that issue."

As the CIA Director left, I drifted off into space thinking about the arrangements being undertaken by a few men to possibly kill me, one man, while an entire army was being used to kill many student protestors. Would change ever come to China? I seriously doubted it simply because of the size of the population and the need for absolute authority by the Chinese government to control their vast population.

Later that day, I was informed that the soon-to-be Vice-President was in place off Massachusetts Avenue at her new residence. Her confirmation should be finalized within the next two days.

Right on schedule, Victoria Wilson was confirmed by the Senate and her swearing in was scheduled for that very evening here at the White House. The Chief Justice of the Supreme Court did the honors and America had a new Vice-President. Her beaming son stood next to her as she took the Oath of Office.

"I, Victoria Wilson, do solemnly swear that I will support and defend the Constitution of the United States against all enemies, foreign and domestic; that I will bear true faith and allegiance to the same; that I take this obligation freely, without any mental reservation or purpose of evasion; and that I will well and faithfully discharge the duties of the office on which I am about to enter: So help me God."

I embraced my new Vice-President and wished her good luck in her new position. I shook her son's hand and a hundred or more photos were taken. America finally had a woman in one of the top two governing positions and second in line to the Presidency. Baby, you've come a long way!

We all proceeded into the East Room of the White House, the largest of the public rooms, where a reception was held for the new Vice-President. About 120 guests were present and light food and champagne was served to all.

"Vicky, enjoy tonight for tomorrow begins work," I said with a smile.

"Oh, I'm under no illusion that this job is all parties and no work. I intend to be in my office in the Executive Office Building bright and early. I apparently have two very thick folders to read on just the essentials regarding security and protocol. Plus, I need to learn my duties as President of the Senate."

"All of which I have complete confidence in you to be able to do. Tonight, just enjoy yourself. Tomorrow will take care of itself."

Just before midnight Vice-President Wilson and her motorcade left the White House for her residence, and the White House shut down for the night. I was exhausted. I said goodnight to my agents, and went to bed.

CHAPTER 11
ASLAM ALAIKUM

It was time for the Middle East summit and Marine One was waiting on the White House lawn to take me to Andrews Air Force Base. The Secret Service was very nervous about this trip and every precaution that they could think of was in place. I really wanted to leave Shane at the White House because I didn't want him in any danger, but he blew a fuse at even the thought of not going.

I received my final intelligence briefing and was handed a personal locater device that would show the Secret Service where I was at all times. I hugged Mary my secretary and kissed my faithful Scottie companion on the head as we headed out of the White House and boarded Marine One for the short flight to Andrews. It was 9:00 P.M. as Marine One took off and I gazed down upon official Washington all lit up at night. It was rather beautiful.

We landed near Air Force One and I immediately went up the stairs and entered the beautiful Presidential jet for the first time. I was met by the Air Force crew including the Brigadier General who was the pilot. As I turned around, my Marine aide Jack was standing there taking my coat from me and greeting me with a smile.

"Good to have you on this trip, Jack."

"Thank you, Mr. President, good to be here with you. Let me show you to your quarters if you like, sir."

I followed the cute blond Marine in his tight uniform to my own cabin which was located in the front of the aircraft. Inside was a queen size bed, dresser, bathroom and shower, television, and a small bar. I was the only one on the plane that would have an actual bed to sleep in, while everyone else had to make do with seats that became somewhat like a bed when properly adjusted. I took off my jacket and tie, and gave them to Jack who hung them up. Since I wasn't ready for bed yet, I decided to watch some television and turned it on in my cabin. A crew member asked me if I wanted anything to eat, and I ordered a sandwich. On this trip, I would eat alone most of the time, as Shane would have to maintain a post.

We took off into the night skies and turned out over the Atlantic Ocean for the long trip to Jordan. We would refuel in Frankfurt, Germany at Ramstein Air Force Base before continuing on to Jordan. After taking a few phone calls and watching a movie, I decided that I was tired enough to go to bed.

I was awoken as we landed in Germany for refueling and went back to sleep before we took off again. I wanted to be as rested as I could for these talks. While I was sleeping, the Secret Service continued to receive a steady stream of updates on the security situation on the ground. We were due to land in Amman within a few hours and massive security measures awaited us.

Jack woke me exactly one hour before we were to land, and I got up quickly, showered, dressed, and had breakfast. I scanned the morning news briefs and read where the Arabs were not happy that this summit was taking place, but we already knew that. Now the general public knew it. Part of what I was given was a decoded transmission from the CIA detailing more of the Saudi involvement in various anti-American plans in operation. One of the plans was to buy their way into port control so that they could regulate to some extent what came into the United States. This contract was being championed by my former opponent for my current job.

"Mr. President, we land in ten minutes and the Secret Service would like to see you."

"Thank you, Jack, ask them to come in."

The Special Agent in charge of my detail and Shane entered my cabin with grim looks on their faces. Shane was carrying, of all things, a rain coat.

"Mr. President, we would like to ask you to wear this raincoat, as it is specially made for you. You will feel that it is extra heavy which is the bullet resistant material used in the entire coat. If you were struck by a bullet wearing this, you would probably suffer broken bones and bruises, but for most of the lower caliber weapons, you would survive the gunshot."

"Well, at least it's black and formal looking. Of course, I don't expect that it's raining by any chance in Amman, is it?"

"No sir, it isn't. Once inside the hotel complex, you can take this off. We would like you to wear it mostly when you're outside. In addition, this other item is like a breast plate that you wear under your shirt. It protects your vital organs from bullet penetration and combined with the raincoat, affords you a much better chance."

"I'd better put that thing on now as we are about to land," I said, removing my shirt and tie to put the vest on and then redressing.

"Sir, we are landing in sixty seconds, please buckle in," advised an Air Force Officer.

Wheels touched down and we were in Amman, Jordan, near the Dead Sea and the site of some of the Biblical stories important to the Christian faith. The schedule called for me to enter an armored limo flown over earlier in the day and ride to a hangar where arrival speeches would be made. From there a motorcade would speed us to the resort where the summit was meeting. When the door to the plane was opened, a wave of hot, dry air swept into the cabin of Air Force One. I looked over at the SAC and gave him a frown over the temperature as it related to me wearing the raincoat.

"Now, sir, after you go out onto the stairway, continue down without stopping. If you have to wave, do it from the steps as you are going down. Hold onto the railing with one hand and wave with the other. Should you fall, there will be an agent in front of you to land on so you won't actually hit the stairs. There is also less of you exposed with agents that close to you. Agent Thompson here will be directly behind you. Once at the bottom, go inside the limo immediately."

"I understand."

The advance agents and a couple of Air Force personnel exited the aircraft first and I followed directly behind, descending the stairs quickly and in the manner advised. When we reached the tarmac, I was whisked into the back of the limo and the motorcade drove the few hundred yards to a hangar where a few hundred well screened people were waiting for my arrival.

There to greet me when I stepped out from the limo was King Hussein of Jordan and his wife, Queen Rania. A host of officials were introduced to me and we moved to the podium where the King and I made short speeches. We finished with an embrace and hopeful predictions for a successful summit.

"Mr. President, I will let you get to the resort, and I will join you this evening for the opening dinner and speech. Should you require anything that our staff cannot get you, call me on my cell phone. Here is my card with the number on it."

"Thank you, Your Majesty, that is most gracious of you. I look forward to seeing you this evening when we might have a little more time to talk."

The King and his wife got into the back of a Mercedes and I entered the cool confines of the Presidential limo. With great fanfare, the motorcade took off towards the resort. At least twenty-four cars made up the motorcade, not including marked Jordanian police cars that blocked off intersections and cleared the way through traffic. Shane told me from the front seat that we were doing in excess of seventy miles per hour and would be at the resort in no more than ten minutes. I didn't really get a chance to see much of the passing countryside because of the speed. When we did slow down it was to enter the Resort compound that had been totally taken over by the summit. We passed through gates that were heavily guarded by Jordanian Army soldiers, who came to attention as we passed, and dozens of police.

"Mr. President, we're going to pull underneath the portico of the hotel. Please stay inside until we okay your exit, and then move quickly. Shane will be right behind you."

"I understand. I trust the rooms have been searched very recently?"

"Yes sir, including secret service dogs brought in just for this. In fact, they will remain in the suite until your arrival."

As the motorcade slowed considerably, I saw that we were turning onto a long driveway that led up to the entrance of the hotel. Police and military personnel were everywhere I looked. The limo came to a halt, and I sat quietly in the rear seat as men moved all around the car and formed almost a corridor into the hotel itself.

Shane nodded to me through the car window, and then opened the door. I got out and quickly moved down the short walkway past the hotel doors in about three seconds. Shane was right behind me as he was supposed to be and in fact had his hand on the small of my back. We went directly to an elevator that was opened and staffed by my agents. Once in, we moved directly without stopping to the Presidential Suite. When the doors opened, I was met by the sight of at least a dozen more Secret Service agents who were responsible for floor and suite security.

Once inside the suite, I began to breathe again and watched as the German Shepherds were led out, having done their job. As hotel suites go, this was an extremely beautiful and opulent one, complete with two levels and three bedrooms, a living room, dining room, full kitchen, piano, televisions in every room, and a beautiful bathroom with a hot tub inside. Attached to the second floor of the suite was an outside sun deck with furniture, which was taken over by my agents. I unpacked with the help of Jack, who accompanied me, and put on clothes that I could relax in until it was time to dress in a business suit for this evening's opening speeches and dinner. I had just over six hours to make final preparations for the event.

As I sat down in the living room, aides and security buzzed all about me doing their jobs. One of the senior CIA people who came with me approached and asked to speak to me.

"Mr. President, we have some further information. It seems that the extensive precautions we have taken have frustrated their attempts to use a sniper to bring you down. It is now our belief that an attempt to kill you by use of a bomb will be their current aim. The dogs will become an even more important tool in your safety than before. We intend to have them at the entrance to the ballroom where the summit dinner will take place. Every one going into the hall will have to go past the dogs. Most upsetting of all, we now possess news that Saudi Arabia had a direct hand in the planned assassination attempt on your life, as well as having learned some details of your visit including classified itinerary."

"Why would the Saudis want me dead, and do we have a leak?"

"Forgive me, sir, but the first reason is that you are gay. The second reason is that they're afraid you'll be able to pull off a deal in the Middle East that will not leave them in charge along with Iran. Finally, it's payback for Bush's war in Iraq, pure and simple. As for the leak, it would appear so, sir."

"Thanks for the information, Roger; let me think on this and in the meantime, find that leak."

Something didn't add up to me. Why would the Saudis risk their major arms supplier and their largest oil customer by killing the President of the United States over a sexual orientation issue? There was a piece missing to the puzzle and hopefully someone would figure out what that piece was.

I heard sirens and went to the window to see what was happening, only to have Shane tell me to stay away from the windows. He looked out and told me it was the Israeli Prime Minister arriving on schedule. According to the records, all parties to the Summit were now on property. I decided to take a short nap as I hadn't slept all that well on the plane.

"Jack, wake me up ninety minutes before I'm due downstairs, will you? And have all my clothes ready, please."

"Yes, Mr. President."

I drifted off to sleep thinking that nothing made much sense about the current situation, but I knew I needed to figure it out.

IN a brightly lit room a few thousand miles away, several men had gathered, drinks in hand. These were the men whose sole aim was to get rid of me and the new Vice-President, clearing the way for the Speaker of the House to assume the White House. They were angry and frustrated that I had been able to have Governor Wilson confirmed so quickly, as it meant they had to carry out two assassinations instead of one, making their aims all the more difficult to accomplish.

"Why didn't our friends in the Senate slow down the confirmation?"

"I understand the President made a good case for getting her swiftly confirmed and they agreed to it. After all, the Senate is a different animal from the House and they are more difficult to control in some respects."

The man in charge spoke for the first time, and the others listened closely. "If our friends in the Middle East fail to kill this guy, then we will have to make sure we do so in the first weeks he is back. Reports indicate due to the amount of security in place for Windsor, our sniper never had a chance to get near him, let alone get off a lethal shot. He must not be allowed to block the port deal or our other business ventures in the Middle East. But in order to insure that the Speaker becomes President, we will have to take out both the President and Vice-President at the same time, which means explosives when they are together. Our first attempt failed, and it shouldn't have. If it wasn't for that damn Secret Service agent, Windsor would be dead now, and we would have things well in hand. We can't afford to miss again."

"Sir, I agree, but it's going to be difficult to get both at the same time, especially if we don't want to kill any friends as collateral damage."

"I can't think of any friend important enough to miss our chance to kill both of our targets simultaneously. Here's my plan to get them together. The Speaker of the House will call for a meeting with the President and Vice-President at Greenbrier resort in White Sulphur Springs, West Virginia to discuss ways to further implement a peace plan for the Middle East. We'll call it a 'political think tank for peace', and invite all the appropriate people for such an event. The President will come in Marine One as well as the Vice-President on Marine Two. We will need the flight plans for both and a skilled group of stinger missile operators to destroy both choppers. This will occur over mountainous terrain and will afford our people ample time to escape the area and into Europe. The Speaker will already be in Greenbrier and can be sworn in as President there. Make a note to have a Federal Judge as part of the group."

"There will be difficult logistics involved, but it's not impossible to pull off. Let's hope that our friends in Jordan succeed. If they do, we will need to move on the Vice-President as soon as we get word that he's dead. Do we still have our moles at the Vice-President's house?"

"Yes. Killing her might not be necessary now that I think of it. A much easier way to get to her would be through her kid, who I understand is gay. We snatch the kid and tell her unless she resigns the Vice-Presidency, her kid will die a horrible death. There's no real need for her to be dead if we can achieve the same result. If that plan isn't feasible or we can't get the kid, we go to the first plan."

"Mr. Smith, that's what I'm looking for; people who think! Outstanding idea, let's make preliminary planning to accomplish that task. I don't know of any mother who wouldn't comply faced with the prospect of oh, say having her son's ears cut off and fed to the alligators, do you?" responded the man in charge. "Now, none of you know it, but I will tell you now. We have someone on the inside with the President himself. In fact, he is with the President in Jordan, and will make an attempt to kill Windsor and escape into the night where our agents will be waiting to help him. In fact, they will actually kill him so that a loose end is tied up and can't be followed back to us. He had a chance once before at Camp David, but was thwarted by a Secret Service agent that Windsor is actually sleeping with!"

The rest of the group showed surprise and wanted details. None were given.

"Anything to add to any of this, Speaker Gorski?"

"No, nothing for now. Let's hope Windsor is killed in the Middle East."

The meeting broke up and everyone left at separate times and took various modes of transportation to get back to their homes.

"MR. PRESIDENT, it's time to go down to the ballroom."

"Thanks, Andy. You have my speech? Any changes?"

"Yes sir, and no, there have been no changes or updates."

Shane moved me towards the door as agents and aides surrounded me at the elevator. We arrived at the second floor, one floor above the ballroom, and got off. From there, we walked down the one flight of stairs to the ground floor, avoiding any kind of surprise had we gotten off at the first floor as would have been expected.. We moved through the hotel lobby and into the short corridor that led to the ballroom, past the secret service dogs that sniffed for any scent of explosives and into the room itself. I was escorted to the head table from where I would address the group, joining other heads of state all ready seated. They got up one by one and shook my hand. The Saudi Prince smiled at me.

"As-salam alaykum, Mr. President."

"Greetings, Prince Bandar, how are you?"

"Fine, Mr. President, and you? How was your long journey from Washington?"

"Very informative to say the least, Bandar."

Once I reached my seat, the host of the summit walked to the microphone.

King Hussein opened the summit with words of encouragement for peace and the cessation of killing in the Middle East. He pled for the lives of all children from all countries as the reason to end the killing that had been going on for thousands of years.

"Here in this room, are the leaders who can make the plans necessary to effect that change, and to do what many others have tried to do but failed. The one example we have of what is possible, is the lasting peace that was struck at the Camp David accords between Israel and Egypt. Much to their credit, there have been no military conflicts between these two countries since that time. We must strive to reach a 'Middle East Accord' that will have the same lasting impact on the region. This goal is all the more important now that nuclear weapons are beginning their proliferation into the Middle East. We have a rare chance here to make lasting history. Thank you, Mr. President, for organizing this summit. May Allah bless it and ensure its success."

The King sat down to the applause of those gathered in the room. When it ceased, it was my turn to speak. The room went silent as I approached the microphone. After a ten minute speech, I ended with a carrot and stick.

"Finally, we have no choice but to make peace in the Middle East. Syria has a nuclear bomb, actually more than one bomb. Others such as Iran are trying to build or buy a bomb. Israel has the bomb. All of the parties in this room are or have been hostile towards Israel or one another at some point in your common history. Some in this room are hostile towards the United States, and yes, the United States is hostile to some in this room. But the ultimate goal of the United States is not to occupy the Middle East, or to 'own' it, but to have genuine, world stabilizing peace throughout this region. In order to have this, we must stop the proliferation of nuclear weapons; stop demanding the end of the state of Israel; and settle factional religious wars amongst nations.

"There is one immutable point that must be understood by all. As long as there is a United States, there will be an Israel. Any nation that seeks to destroy Israel, will be destroyed itself in the end. Any nation that launches a nuclear attack on Israel or on an ally of the United States will itself be uninhabitable for tens of thousands of years. There is no real choice but peace. Any country that would dare attempt an assassination of the leader of another nation will pay consequences beyond its imagination. Even the plotting of such an assassination could lead to irreparable harm to the relations between the affected countries.

"With all the needs of the people of the Middle East, think of what could be accomplished with the oil wealth of those here assembled to make a better life for your people. Why waste billions of petrol dollars on offensive weapons that cannot be used without assuring your own destruction? Learn from the mistakes of the cold war between the United States and the Soviet Union. We wasted tens of billions on the ability to destroy each other dozens of times over. The race bankrupted the Soviet Union, and kept the American public from advances in medical science that could have cured cancer. This cure could have had an effect not only on the people of the United States, but the people of the world. Is this what you all really want? Think about it. What could you accomplish working together instead of against one another? Issues that exist between Israel and others can be worked out if you approach the table with an open mind and a willingness to give as well as take. There is no other answer. If you turn a deaf ear to this summit, then you are condemning your own people to a life of misery. It is in all of your hands."

The end of my speech brought loud applause from Jordan and Israel, weaker applause from Egypt and Iraq, and almost no applause from Syria and Iran. I expected nothing more or less. Each of the other heads of state rose and spoke, blaming tensions in the region on Israel and the United States, with the exception of Jordan and Israel; even the Egyptians made mention of the military presence in Iraq of the United States as a factor keeping the region hot, a fact that I could not entirely dismiss as false.

The session ended four hours after it began, with no new agreements reached. It was now time for lower staffs to attempt to work out something to agree upon. I had no illusions that Iran, Saudi Arabia, or Syria wanted peace with Israel, or apparently the United States. If no progress was shown by the next afternoon, I would go back to Washington.

By 9:30, no breaking news was reported to me so I decided to turn in early. Jack followed me into the bedroom and asked me if anything was wrong.

"Ah, Jack, it's an old back injury and I've got some moderate pain tonight. There are a couple of discs in my back that are close to being a major problem."

"Sir, might I recommend a shower and then a massage? I believe that will help you to sleep better."

"I don't think the Secret Service would take kindly to my calling up the hotel masseur for a massage."

"You don't have to, sir. Before I joined the Corps, I was a certified massage therapist. I would be happy to work on your back, sir, and try to bring you some relief."

"You're kidding? You are certified in massage? Did I get a bargain or what when I picked you to come to work for me?"

"If I might say so myself, sir, yes, you did," the Marine replied with a large grin.

"Very well, I'll take a shower now. See if you can find anything around here that resembles any kind of lotion or oil."

As the hot water ran over my body, my thoughts drifted to the young stud of a Marine who would soon be rubbing my back with his muscular hands. I found myself getting aroused at the thought of it. I reprimanded myself for even thinking of Jack in a sexual way. He was merely serving the President as best he could. Hmm, I could think of a couple ways he could serve me.... I turned the water off, shook like my Scottie when she was wet, and opened the shower curtain to once again be surprised by Jack standing there with a towel.

"Damn it, Marine; stop scaring the shit out of me like this. I just don't expect to open the curtain and find a man standing there with a towel! One of these times, I'm going to let out a howl and the Secret Service are going to run in here and shoot your ass!"

"Oh, I'm sorry, sir, I didn't think. In the barracks, I guess you get use to other men being around when you are naked in the bathroom. Sorry sir, it won't happen again."

All I could do at that point was laugh out loud. "No, I'm sorry, Jack, for being such a school girl over it. You're right, of course. I'll get use to it, don't worry," I said as I dried off.

I walked out into the bedroom and asked, "Jack, what should I put on for this?"

"Sir, just lay down on the bed and drape the towel across your buttocks. As you can see, I retrieved a pair of gym shorts to put on which will allow me more freedom to move about on your back. Excuse me while I change over here."

I laid down on the bed and put the towel over my ass, watching out of the corner of my eye as Jack stripped off his uniform. His build was incredible and the bulge in his shorts was mouth watering. For my second shock in the last three minutes, Jack stripped off his underwear before putting on his gym shorts. I didn't even try and look away as this beautiful young stud was briefly in all his naked glory. Jack looked up as he stepped into his shorts and caught me looking at his cock.

"I'm sorry, Jack; I didn't mean to stare at you."

"Ha, that's okay, Mr. President. After all, I've seen you naked more than twice, as you know. Now, I can get on top of your lower back and work down with my hands – it's far more effective that way."

Jack climbed onto my back and sat down on top of my ass. The tip of his cock that hung out one side of his shorts brushed briefly against my lower back. I felt myself getting hard underneath the towel and fought that happening any further. Jack was true to his word; the massage was not amateur in nature but used techniques taught in class. His hands were magnificent and I could feel the relief pouring into my back. As I was drifting off into bliss, a knock on the door startled both of us, and before I could say anything Shane entered the room, closing the door behind him. A look of shock or betrayal crossed his handsome brow. Jack got off my back and stood by the side of the bed.

"Excuse me, Mr. President, I didn't know you were, ah, engaged."

"It's okay, Agent, Jack was just giving me a massage and was working up to my neck when you entered."

Shane approached the bed looking at me and ignoring Jack all together. Could he be jealous? Before I could get myself together, Shane had Jack on the floor with his gun pressed firmly to his head.

"If you move, motherfucker, I'll blow your brains out all over the carpet and not even think twice about it, do we understand each other?"

"Shane, stop at once! What the fuck is wrong with you?"

Shane ignored me and spoke into his mic. "Okay, subject down."

My bedroom door burst open and at least six more agents entered the room with guns drawn. I was totally flustered and didn't know what to say as Jack was handcuffed and hauled out of my room with his feet never touching the floor.

Only Shane remained in the room. "What in the fuck is going on, Shane?"

"Mr. President, we just received word from the NSA that your little Marine Sergeant was in fact a participant in the plot to kill you. You said he was working his way up to your neck? I'm not surprised since he planned on killing you!"

"Don't be ridiculous! Intelligence has to be wrong on this. Hell, he was just a nobody at Camp David until I noticed him and brought him along!"

"Yes sir, a gay Marine just happened to be at Camp David when the new President who happens to be gay arrived for his first visit to the Camp. His orders were to kill you at Camp David, but he picked up on your apparent sexual interest in him and decided to ride along with you to see how far he could go. Well, it got him inside the White House, and almost killed you. If I hadn't burst in when I did, you would be dead now in all likelihood, and the Marine would be gone in the night somewhere."

I got off the bed, letting the towel drop to the floor, and gave Shane a quick kiss and a hug. This was the second time the man had saved my Presidential ass. I quickly got dressed and entered the living room area to find out what had happened since Jack was taken away.

"Okay, brief me, what the fuck is going on with that Marine? Who is he working with?"

Everyone in the room appeared ashen faced. "What's wrong, don't tell me he escaped!"

"No, Mr. President, he didn't escape in the usual way. He committed suicide."

"Excuse me? He what? How in the fuck did he kill himself when he was in handcuffs and surrounded by fifty agents?"

"Old KGB trick, sir. He had a cyanide capsule in one of the dental caps in his mouth. He broke the cap off, the pill dropped into his mouth, and he bit on it and was gone before he hit the floor. There was nothing we could do about it."

"This is like a fucking nightmare. The Arabs are trying to kill me, and now a United States Marine was going to try and do the job for them? Gentlemen, I want answers and fast. Who is behind this? Who got to a Marine with his kinds of clearances, clearances that got him next to the President?"

"On top of him, as I hear it," snickered one agent under his breath.

Before I could process what I and everyone else in the room heard, Shane was on top of the agent, propelling him out of the room and into their command post. The Agent in Charge was right behind Shane.

"Mr. President, none of the rest of us feel that this is a matter for humor and we apologize for Adams' comment. He's a jerk and is gone from here, you'll never see him again," said one of the senior agents who I didn't really know.

"Thank you...." I turned around and went back into the bedroom to think.

A few minutes later, Shane knocked on the door and entered. He closed the door and came over and put his arms around me.

"David, I'm sorry you heard that asshole's comment. He was relieved of duty and is at this very moment being sent back to Washington to be dismissed from the Service."

"I guess in a way I had it coming. What the fuck was I thinking?"

"Maybe you were thinking with your dick?"

I didn't respond to the comment from Shane. After all, he was right. I could have gotten someone from medical services that traveled with me all the time to give me a massage or something to relax my muscles, but I chose the young available 'honey pot', which is what former KGB agents who were working the sex angle were called. Fuck, I was stupid, and it almost cost me my life and great trauma to the American people. I swore to myself then and there, never again. I would limit any sexual interest that might surface to Shane and Shane only. Whether Shane realized it or not, he had just become my only lover.

The Agent in Charge and Andy came into the bedroom to advise me that everything was secure and that there was no progress to report from the staff work being done. It was suggested that everyone turn in to be rested for the next round with the heads of state in the morning. I agreed and said goodnight. Tonight, I wanted to be able to hold Shane all night, but of course I was unable to do so. I went to bed, and Shane went off duty and to his bedroom on the other side of the living room.

At exactly three o'clock in the morning, I was awoken by the sounds of gunfire and explosions coming from outside the hotel. The Secret Service rushed into my room and got me out of bed and into a bathroom on the other side of the suite away from the gunfire. I was told by the agents surrounding me to lie down in the bathtub, which would provide extra protection from gunshots.

"What the hell is going on now?"

"We don't know anything, Mr. President, other than Jordanian forces have engaged some kind of raiding party that landed by sea. They are trying to fight their way to the hotel," the head of my security detail said in a somewhat shaky voice.

Just as Shane came into my new location, an RPG-29 rocket hit the windows of the master bedroom where I had lay sleeping only moments before. The inside of the room was totally destroyed along with the wall that separated the bedroom from the living room, killing three Secret Service Agents immediately. Flames broke out as bedding, curtains and carpet caught on fire. A full security alert was called and I was ordered to prepare to evacuate into the motorcade at a moment's notice. My military aide who had the 'football' was unharmed and by my side. Water sprinklers had gone off to fight the fires that now consumed my former bedroom.

All classified documents were accounted for and secured as I was ordered to move out. Over forty-five agents and staff moved into elevators and staircases to descend to the garage level of the hotel. Since all of the cars of the motorcade were under constant protection by the Service, they were assumed safe and I was placed into the back of Limo One. Chaos reigned supreme all around the hotel as Jordanian Army units engaged about a hundred terrorists and were gaining the upper hand. When they had been pushed back to the opposite side of the hotel from us, orders were given to move out and head for Air Force One. I received a phone call from King Hussein who expressed his regrets and offered his military to guarantee my safety. I thanked him but told him we were taking evasive maneuvers and I would call him back shortly. I didn't feel comfortable telling him on a cell phone that we were heading for my plane.

The back of my limo held Andy Carter and five heavily armed Agents with automatic weapons, including Shane. My usual limo driver agent was at the wheel and when we moved out, it was fast and furious. We were led by a single Jordanian police car that was told only after we left where we were heading. Two agents were riding in that vehicle and told him not to use the radio, but just to escort us as fast as possible to the hangar. Our Air Force crew was wakened and told to make Air Force One ready to leave. A request had just been forwarded to Jordanian Air Force personnel to have fighters take off with our plane and to escort us out of the immediate area.

I made a secure call from the limo phone back to Washington, informing the Vice-President what had happened and that we were evacuating the area. As I finished the call, we arrived at the airport. The motorcade swung closely to the hangar where Air Force One was just emerging from in the dark. I remained in the car for another five minutes and then was briskly escorted aboard the plane, whose engines were starting up even as I took off the coat I was wearing over my pajamas. The second Air Force plane was brought out that would carry the limos and associated personnel out of the region. They had landed twelve hours before I had arrived in Jordan.

As I took my seat and was secured into it by Air Force personnel, the jet began its climbing maneuver while releasing anti-missile devices the plane carried. In fact both Air Force planes were doing the same, which was an extra precaution since we had six Jordanian fighter jets escorting us. No one took a shot at us, however, and our exit was successful. I was told later that the enemy would not have expected us to immediately depart from Jordan but to stay and try to save face. Once we were safely airborne, reports began to arrive from our former location. All terrorists had been killed by the Jordanians and no other head of state was targeted. The terrorists were members of the al-Sadr Brigade. I was not surprised by that information.

"Andy, tell the pilot to make for London. We're going to see another King, one I know we can trust."

I picked up a phone next to my seat and told the Air Force communications officer to put me through to Buckingham Palace and attempt to get the King on the phone. We would land at Heathrow, and then the planes would be flown to RAF Bentwaters Air Force Base which was American occupied and controlled. It was only twenty minutes by flight from London and the base had a secured air field with tons of security police.

My phone buzzed and I picked it up. "Mr. President, I have the King of England on the phone."

"Sorry to disturb you, William, but this is rather urgent."

"Of course, cousin, no problem. How is Jordan?"

"Well, at the moment rather hot. Some bunch of needledicks just tried to blow me up, so we packed our good china and the silver, and left the bloody country. Mind terribly if we come visit a few days early?"

"No, of course not. It might upset the plans of my protocol department, but they'll get over it. How soon will you be here?"

"We should be at Heathrow in about five hours. Could you notify your security people and all, I'm afraid my limo and other things are in a second plane that will land after we are already on the ground."

"Not to worry. I'll have suitable cars for you and your people waiting at the VIP terminal and get you over here to Buckingham in a jiffy. Once inside these gates, you will be safe, cousin. I'll get to work on this straight away."

"Thanks so much, William. I do hate to be a bother, but the damn Arabs just won't give peace a chance."

"See you very soon, David, and look forward to it. By the way, you will of course be guests here at the Palace so don't worry about hotels and all that. This big old drafty place could use a group like yours in here."

"Good show, cousin, 'til we meet."

I signaled Andy Carter to join me which he did, bringing along two cups of coffee.

"Andy, tell everyone we are headed to England, and that we will be staying at Buckingham Palace. Get our security people on this right away. Have them get in touch with the Palace and coordinate everything through there. Let the Captain know that we will follow a guide truck to a VIP area at Heathrow."

"I'll get right on it and I will also advise State."

I went into my cabin to see what clothes I had with me on the plane, since all that I had in Jordan was now ash. I was able to determine that I had suitable clothes but would more than likely have to go shopping at Harrods to pick up another suit and a couple of shirts and underwear. How embarrassing to arrive in Great Britain, cousin to the King of England, as practically a refugee in need of clothing. Someone was going to pay for this and pay dearly.

"Mr. President, King Hussein on the red phone for you, sir."

"President Windsor here, Your Majesty."

"Mr. President, I again want to apologize for the assault on your presence here in my country. As you have been informed, all attackers were killed by our Army and our intelligence service is looking into their origins and any other information we can ascertain. The other heads of state have agreed to stay on throughout today in talks. This is a hopeful sign since they didn't just leave after you left."

"Yes, I should imagine all are pretty safe with the exception of the Israeli Prime Minister. Is he secured so that no one can get to him while he remains there?"

"Yes sir, although his accommodations are no longer regal, they are secure. I have taken personal command of his security and will see it he leaves here as he arrived, alive."

"Thank you, King Hussein. As you know, his assassination would light the fuse that would lead to devastation in the Middle East; a devastation that I fear would also consume you and your great country."

"Yes, it is true what you speak. I have told all of the heads of state that any nation responsible for such an act would be considered an enemy of Jordan henceforth. I don't anticipate any attempts from them; but this al-Sadr group, they are another thing altogether."

"I ask Your Majesty if you would keep me informed of any progress towards peace. I will not be returning to the United States but will stay a couple of days in Europe. Good luck with your mission, Your Majesty."

"Thank you, Mr. President, and praise be to Allah that you are safe."

I changed into one of the two backup suits that were still with me on the plane as it would be just over three hours before we landed and I knew I could not sleep. Afterwards, I went into the dining area of Air Force One, and had what amounted to lunch. I was joined by Andy Carter, my press spokesman, and John Merriweather who held the title of Presidential advisor.

"Well, guys, I have a sinking suspicion here. There have been two attempts by Americans to kill me, one of them a fucking Marine, and one by an Iraqi Militia group. They have to be working together somehow. Who wants to get rid of me so bad?"

"I am as baffled as you are. But it is evident that you can't go anywhere without a very heavy security presence," said Merriweather. "I would suggest that the CIA and all government intelligence agencies devote maximum effort to figuring this thing out before it's too late."

"I agree, Mr. President. In fact, let's get the CIA liaison in here right now for an update," suggested Carter.

The CIA liaison entered our small room after being buzzed by Andy Carter. He had with him a folder marked 'Top Secret.'

"Please update us on the situation as it relates to these attempts to kill me since day one."

"Mr. President, we are starting to get a picture that frankly is very scary. With the attempt by the Marine to kill you, followed shortly by the attack on the hotel, we believe that there is a definite link to home grown terrorists. But, these home grown types are not what you might imagine. It took a lot of connections and finesse to get that Marine planted at Camp David, and then to get him to have you pick him for your enlisted aide de camp; even more so than getting an assassin into the Capitol on Inauguration Day. The initial leads indicate the involvement of powerful corporate interests, interests that might be afraid of you cutting off their supply of war profits as well as other sources of government income. We believe that your being gay is being used as a smoke screen for the real reasons behind these attempts. If this proves out to be right, then it is possible that they have essentially 'employed' the al-Sadr Brigade as contract killers to get you in the Middle East. Unfortunately, sir, you should expect more attempts on your life as they will not stop until they succeed or we identify them and put them out of business."

"Well, my own preference would be for you to put them out of business at the end of a rope! I can't believe they would go this far to achieve their monetary goals."

"Sir, we have known for a long time that President Kennedy was killed not by Oswald, who was a dupe they used, but by unseen forces unhappy with both his and Bobby's attempts to put the mob out of business, as well as cheat the mob out of money that was promised for the Bay of Pigs attempt. Money was surely at the base of the plot to kill the Kennedy brothers."

"What are you all doing to find out who is behind this?"

"Sir, we have in custody associates of the Marine, and we are interrogating them to find out how he got close to you. They are resisting our attempts and you will receive a request shortly from Langley to give us permission to use extraordinary methods to elicit the needed information, as we do not practice rendition any longer."

"In other words, you want my okay to torture these associates, is that correct?"

"In short, yes sir."

"Well, tell Langley not to even bother sending me such a request as I would deny it. There has to be another way to get them to talk. Is there enough evidence against these men that prove they are part of a conspiracy to assassinate me?"

"Yes, sir."

"Then convene a general court martial now, tonight, and prosecute them. If a jury of their peers convicts them, execute them one at a time until the remaining ones agree to talk. This way it is legal, no torture, and an end to the traitors. If they talk, commute their sentences to life in prison and send the cases to me for final review for any possible reductions. Conduct the court martials in complete secrecy, but make sure they have lawyers."

"Yes sir, I will send out the order now."

"Get me the Chairman of the Joint Chiefs of Staff on the phone."

A few minutes later the Chairman was on the phone. "General Gates, I want you to order an immediate redeployment of half of our troops in Iraq to Afghanistan, and bring home the rest. Those soldiers who have served more than two tours are to come home. Once things get settled down, eliminate all National Guardsmen from the combat force in the Middle East. It's time to bring George Bush's folly to a close. And by the way, I want as little as possible left behind in Iraq as it pertains to our equipment. Unless it's total junk, it is to be brought home or sent to the other theater of war. Any questions, General?"

"Yes sir, two. What is our goal in Afghanistan, and are we really just dumping Iraq altogether? Remember, we have permanent bases under construction."

"Our goal in Afghanistan is to stabilize the country as much as possible, eliminate as much of the Taliban as we can, find and kill Bin Laden, and finally, destroy every opium crop you can find. As for Iraq, yes, we are getting the hell out of there. Cease all construction with the exception of a fortified embassy. I want severe oversight of everything being done at the embassy, and if it is a mess now, tear it down and build it right. Any other questions, General?"

"No sir, it will take at least forty-eight hours to begin to implement your orders."

"Very well, General, I want progress reports."

CHAPTER 12
BANGERS AND CHIPS

Air Force One rolled to a stop in front of the VIP hangar terminal that was usually reserved for the Royal Family as well as visiting heads of state. I was ready to go as soon as the door was cracked, heading down the stairs swiftly and into the waiting British supplied cars. Mine was the same car used by the King: a 2010 armored Bentley. Our small motorcade left Heathrow en route to the Palace at a high rate of speed with at least a dozen London special police units in escort, as well as forty-seven Secret Service Agents jammed into much smaller cars than they were used to operating in.

As the sun was just rising, traffic had yet to become heavy and we sliced through the streets quickly, entering the front gates of Buckingham Palace in under twenty minutes. The gates were open and heavily guarded by local police carrying automatic weapons. We pulled around to the rear of the Palace which was secluded and hidden, and there King William, my cousin, waited for my arrival. I got out of the Bentley, shook William's hand and then hugged him.

"Welcome to my home, Mr. President. I'm sorry you have had to arrive under such circumstances, but I can assure you, you will be quite comfortable and safe here."

"Thank you, Your Majesty, for your hospitality and welcome. I look forward to talking with you at your convenience."

The King turned to indicate we should move inside and we walked up the red carpet and into the Palace that has stood the test of both history and time. Most famous buildings that you see on television are much smaller in person; that wasn't the case with the Palace. The rooms were enormous and elegant. It was obvious that great care was taken to keep the Royal main palace in top shape.

We entered what was the ceremonial reception room for heads of state where a tray of champagne was waiting for us. Even though it was morning, both William and I had been up for hours so it wasn't as awful as it might sound to drink champagne at 7:30 in the morning.

"Mr. President, please indulge us in a brief welcoming ceremony. I would like to toast the arrival of my dear cousin from America who also happens to be President of the United States, and to state that we are delighted at his presence here in London. We were horrified at the news of his forced escape from the attack in Jordan by those who hate freedom and will do anything to prevent its spread. To the President!"

Everyone took a sip of their champagne and I returned the toast.

"May I now offer a toast to the King of England, who also happens to be my dear cousin, and to his hospitality, and to the friendship that is lifelong between our two nations. Long may it live, long live the King!"

After everyone drained their glasses, we were shown to our respective rooms by the Royal household staff. I was taken to my quarters by William and found it to be a suite just down the hall from the King's bedroom.

"I hope this will be satisfactory, David. There is an attached bedroom for the wife of the dignitary who sleeps in this room, which is actually quite rare. In your case, you could have one of your aides or bodyguards stay in that room. Is this acceptable?"

"More than acceptable, cousin, it is incredible. Such beauty and elegance. Shane, would you care to take that bedroom?"

"Yes, Mr. President."

"Well then, would you like to get some rest so that you are refreshed for the state dinner tonight?"

"State dinner? You had such short notice, are you sure? I won't' be offended at the least if we dispense with that protocol."

"Cousin, your state dinner has been fully planned and prepared for already; all we did was move it up two days. It is nothing and it is scheduled for eight o'clock this evening, if that meets with your approval?"

"Yes, of course it does. I will be honored to attend and I look forward to it. However, I will need to dash off to Harrods as all of my clothes with few exceptions were destroyed in the hotel attack. I can't go in something like this."

"Nonsense, we will have Harrods come here to the Palace. Does your staff have all your measurements? Do you need shoes, the whole thing?"

"That would be awesome, William, as I do represent my country and don't feel comfortable with only the clothes left on my plane. Yes, Andy Carter can give your staff all of my sizes, and he also knows my tastes. I would like to try and get four solid undisturbed hours of sleep, and then I should be on my feet."

"Good show. I'll have this seen to at once. When you wake up, you will have several styles of everything you require to chose from, and what you don't chose will be sent back. Harrods will not be told that the clothes are for you, just as an extra security measure, not that I don't trust Harrods with the entire Palace! Can I have anything sent up to this room prior to your turning in?"

"Just one thing if you can manage it, and I apologize for asking it: could I get a large bottle of diet 7-up? I love the taste and I take my two pills with it."

"I'm sure we have it as your preferences were seen to by the kitchen staff a couple of weeks ago. Now get some rest and I'll have you woken at say, twelve o'clock?"

"That would be great, William, thank you."

I gave him a hug and told him I was pleased to be with family in England and that I appreciated the extra trouble he was going through on my behalf. Shane reported in to the SAC to inform him of the sleeping arrangements and that 'Condor One' was going to sleep for four hours. He said he would remain close to Condor. You bet he would, I thought to myself. I needed him close to me.

The soda arrived, and I had a glass and got into bed. Shane had intended to stay awake and I urged him to join me in the beautiful 'King size' bed. He walked over and locked the door to both his room and mine. He removed his gun and clothes and climbed into my bed with an exhausted look on his face.

"No sex, Shane, just rest. Hold me, please."

"I will gladly do that, David. It's been a bitch of a day and it's only just starting. We were lucky to get out of that hotel room, real lucky."

"Shh, I don't want to talk about anything but how beautiful you look. You are so handsome, Shane. I love it when you are near me."

"Well, I obviously feel the same way around you, David. You really are a special man in your own right, aside from being President."

"Shane, I don't mean to scare you, but I love you. I love you and I am *in* love with you."

A tear formed in the eyes of the man I now knew I loved. Then he spoke: "I've been hoping to hear those words come from your mouth for weeks now. In all honesty, I have been so attracted to you since day one on the campaign trail, and then to have you pick me for the White House detail was beyond my dreams. I love you and want to be with you always."

We kissed for what seemed like an hour. Not the sexual kind of kiss, but the deep passion of the soul kind of kiss, the one that told you that the other person loved you. It was all so surreal; here we were declaring our love for each other, in a bed in Buckingham Palace in London, just down the hall from the King of England. I felt like I was in some kind of Shakespearean play or more appropriately, an Oscar Wilde novel.

We held each other tightly as if we were afraid the other person would simply vanish, our breathing rapid, our bodies hot to the touch. His skin never felt so soft, yet firm and masculine. My hand wandered down his back and over his butt, feeling the curve, the texture, the hardness of his body. I felt something that I had not felt in years;

contentment and security of the soul. This was the man for me; could it last forever like some fairytale?

"Let's get to sleep, and then we can talk about all this later today. Goodnight, my love," I whispered to Shane. His reaction was to snuggle even closer to me. I fell asleep in moments in the arms of the man I loved.

WE slept soundly until a knock on the door woke us both. Shane got out of bed and put on a bathrobe that had been supplied to us both, answering my door as if he had come from the other bedroom. I pretended to be still asleep.

"Pardon me, sir, but I was told to wake the President precisely at noon. It is now that time, sir."

"Yes, thank you for being punctual."

"Sir, dial nine-two-two on the phone and the merchandise from Harrods which arrived over an hour ago will be brought into the President's suite for him to look over and make his selections."

"Yes, will do, thank you."

Shane closed and relocked the door. He came over to the bed and looked down on me with a smile. "It's time to get up so that you can go shopping here in the room. All the stuff from the store is here for you to select from. Now get up, you lazy cow!"

I burst out laughing at Shane's use of a very English expression. "Lazy cow indeed, I will have you know, sir, that I am the President of the United States."

"Yeah, and I'm the King of England!"

"No, he's across the hallway!"

We both laughed and rolled around on the bed like we were two school boys at summer camp. As I realized that the clothes would be arriving, I jumped out of bed naked and threw on a palace robe. I went into the bathroom to comb my hair, brush my teeth, and shave. Another knock at the bedroom door meant no shower at the moment.

When Shane opened the door, there were no less than sixteen footmen holding all manner of boxes and suit bags standing in the hallway. Shane motioned them to come in, and they placed all of the items neatly in a row on the floor. They turned and left without a word. The King's secretary then made an appearance and greeted both Shane and me.

"Good afternoon, Mr. President, I'm Willard, the King's personal secretary." He turned towards Shane and said simply, "Sir," as a way of acknowledging Shane's presence. "These, Mr. President, are the things you require for your wardrobe. All items are from Harrods and all you have to do is select what you like, and leave the rest on the floor. Those items will be collected and returned whence they came. We will then get with your man here, and ensure that you are satisfied with everything. One of the suit bags contains a variety of evening wear for this evening's state dinner. If they are not acceptable, let me know personally, sir."

"Thank you ,Willard, I shall attend to this immediately. By the way, this is Agent Shane Thompson of the United States Secret Service and my personal bodyguard."

"A pleasure, sir. I apologize for assuming you were the President's valet, as you are after all standing here in a bathrobe. Who shall I talk with regarding your affairs, sir?"

"Please talk with Andy Carter; he is my Chief of Staff."

"Of course, Mr. President, and now I shall leave you to go over these things."

After Willard had closed the door, Shane minced his way over to me and said, "I apologize for assuming you were the President's valet, as you are after all standing here in a battttth robe." Shane emphasized the word bath with the suitable English accent. I burst out laughing and said, "Don't be offended, apparently the King's bodyguards don't sleep with him!"

I felt like a kid at Christmas time going through the things sent over by Harrods. Every item without exception was handsome in its own right. I selected four pairs of underwear, socks, and shirts. I chose two pair of pants, a suit, and a tuxedo for the evening. Naturally shoes were chosen to go with the tux or the suit, and a couple of ties rounded off things nicely. I dressed in one of the suits and looked at myself in a full length mirror. I looked like a million bucks and realized just how crappy my own suits looked as compared to the suits from Harrods.

Shane came in from his room and looked me up and down and whistled. "Wow, you look like a million bucks!"

"Actually, I think I look more like a million pounds sterling."

"How much did the stuff you chose cost?"

"I'm not sure; there were no price tags on anything. So, I chose what I liked and what I thought I would look good in, and here we are."

Andy knocked on the door and came in after I boomed the command to enter. Andy looked me over and proclaimed that I was fit and presentable anywhere in polite society. I smiled, saying, "Yeah, it took the King of England to make me look good, huh?"

"Why no, Mr. President, you always look good."

"Brown noser," mumbled Shane with a smile.

"Only to the boss, Agent Thompson, only to the boss. But in this case, it happens to be true."

"Andy, will you tell the King's secretary that the rest of this can go back, and get a bill for what I have kept, while you're at it?."

"Of course, sir. By the way, you have an invitation to lunch with the King at one o'clock. An escort will meet you and take you to the King if you accept."

"Please inform the King I would be delighted. By the way, Andy, I looked out the window and believe I saw about a million press people on the other side of the fence. Is that normal?"

"No sir, they know you are here so the world's press is here as well. Air Force One was seen landing, and well, they figured out the rest with relative ease. You really should issue a statement to the press regarding Jordan."

"Okay, have something drawn up and I'll look at it after lunch." Andy nodded and left.

"Shane, has a command post been set up and have there been any issues with the Brits?"

"Yes sir, the command post is one floor above this and we have the best cooperation that you can imagine. They really are going way out of their way to accommodate all this commotion."

"Good, I'll be sure to thank my cousin at lunch, then. I trust you are coming with me?"

"We might be in a palace owned by your cousin, but you don't go anywhere without me or another agent."

"Well, you'd better report the plans that have been made to the command post while I put the rest of these clothes away."

I had just finished closing the last drawer in the dresser when the escort arrived to take me to lunch. Shane as usual opened the door, and we found a butler wearing a powdered wig standing there, who bowed and said, "Would you follow me, Mr. President, for lunch with His Majesty?"

I left the room with not only Shane in tow, but three other agents as well. I found the Secret Service stationed throughout the palace as we walked for another four minutes, until we came to an open air area at the rear of the palace that was surrounded by a high wall of American boxwood bushes that were at least fifteen feet high. This allowed us to lunch outside on the palace grounds in total privacy as well as security. Even so, the Secret Service was all over the grounds. As I approached the table, the King rose to greet me:

"Good afternoon, Mr. President, you look a lot better now than you did when you arrived this morning."

"Thank you, Your Majesty, I feel a lot better now than when I arrived. Also thanks to Harrods department store for clothing that is far more presentable for the Palace."

"I'm glad to hear it, David. My Secretary informed me that your Chief of Staff requested a bill from Harrods for the clothing you kept. There will be no bill, David, as Harrods took a guess that the clothes were for you, and they sent them with their compliments as a representation of Great Britain and our haberdashery. They have asked for nothing in return, but don't be surprised if sometime in the future a picture of you in one of their suits pops up somewhere with the pronouncement that Harrods even dresses the President of the United States."

"That is rather generous of them, William. I must send them a thank you note. Might I use Palace stationary for that purpose? I should think they would be thrilled at my signature on that letterhead."

"Of course, that's brilliant. They will love it over there. Now shall we eat?"

THE day passed into evening and the state dinner hosted by his Majesty King William V took place with a very select group of people joining us. All of the finest of dinner ware along with the best of foods were used for this occasion. I was very overwhelmed at what the Palace managed to do two days early and with such perfection. The customary toasts were exchanged, with a pledge to continue the close friendship between our two countries, and the dinner broke up just after 11:30. The evening had gone off without a hitch. I had a feeling that everything went off without a hitch around the Palace.

As I got ready to retire with Shane for the night, I had a visit from my CIA liaison. I knew at this time of night, it could not be good news.

"Forgive me for coming to you at this late hour, sir, but I have rather disturbing news that is quite frankly nearly unbelievable."

"Well sir, you have my attention now, what is it?"

"Through the use of Federal wire taps, we have begun to learn the identities of the domestic traitors who are working so hard to not only kill you, but upset your foreign policy agenda. The apparent ringleader is 82 year old Gerry McNealy, the CEO of Xorcet Industries, a multi-billionaire who has millions in defense contracts pending for his companies. But that's not the shocker: we identified one of the co-conspirators on the wire tap by voice analysis and we believe it to be none other than the Speaker of the House of Representatives, Gorski."

"I don't believe it. The Speaker of the House? There hasn't been a case of treason like this since the days of Benedict Arnold! I want proof that it was Gorski on that call, and I want more details. What were they talking about?"

"Sir, they were trying to be discreet, but essentially they were distressed that the Marine failed in his attempt to kill you, followed by the unsuccessful attack of the al-Sadr Brigade. They hinted at one final attempt upon your return to America. We have nothing further than that so far."

"Incredible! The fucking Speaker of the House involved in a plot to kill the President. But wait, that wouldn't do them much good with Wilson being Vice-President, unless Wilson was also to be assassinated. Shane, I want you to relay to the Secret Service Command to double the number of agents on the VP detail, and to secure her down. Oh, and her son too!"

"Yes, Mr. President."

"Anything else from the CIA?"

"No, sir, but we should have confirmation on not only the Speaker, but the others on the phone call."

"Do we know how they plan their 'final' attempt to kill me?"

"No, sir, nothing on that just yet."

As the door closed and Andy Carter left Shane and I alone, I just muttered to myself about the state of America. "The country really went to hell under Bush, incredible."

"I'm going to run up to the command post, will you be all right?"

"Shane, if I'm not safe in Buckingham Palace, then I'm not safe anywhere. Go, take care of business."

I poured a glass of Bailey's Irish Cream on the rocks and got into bed, sipping it as I thought the entire situation over in my mind. How could such an array of forces have come together with the aim of changing the government once again through violence? Would I be another JFK? Would Shane be killed while protecting me? I was startled as the phone next to the bed rang.

"Mr. President, I have the Vice-President on the phone for you."

"Yes, thank you, put her through please."

"Hello, David?"

"Yes, Vicky, is anything wrong?"

"You tell me, David; what looks like an entire regiment of agents and other personnel have just converged on my residence. This place looks like an armed camp preparing for a revolution. What's going on?"

"Vicky, you're going to have to trust me. I've ordered your detail doubled, which includes your son. When I land, I will tell you in person everything I know. Until then, consider yourself under lock-down protection."

"When are you returning?"

"That is going to be decided at the last second. You will be notified when I'm about to land at Andrews. We'll meet as soon as we can get together after that."

"Okay, David, I don't like all this tension and cloak and dagger stuff. Get home safe!"

"Will do, Vicky. Have a good day there in Washington."

I drained my glass as Shane entered the room. "I've taken care of the VP's increase in protection among other things."

"I know. I just had a call from her, freaking out. We need to leave for D.C. tomorrow. In fact, I'll call Andy now so he can begin the arrangements."

That night Shane and I made passionate love, being careful not to make any noise that would give away our nocturnal activities. Each time I made love to Shane, I felt that he was the man I wanted to be with forever and he made me feel emotionally secure. It wasn't just the sex, even though it was fantastic; it was the feelings conveyed during the acts of love making. We each told each other how much we thought we were falling in love.

"How can you truly be my lover, Shane, as a member of the Secret Service? Would you consider leaving your job?"

"Why can't we have both? Why do I have to stop protecting you because I love you?"

"You more than most people should know that love clouds one's judgment. I don't want you getting hurt because you acted differently because we are involved. Why not leave the Service and take an appointment as a Presidential aide? If I should manage to stay alive through two terms, you would have enough time in service when I leave office to retire. Would that be so bad?"

"Do I have to decide now?"

"No, of course not. Let's get to sleep because tomorrow is going to be a rough day and very long."

THE next day I said my goodbyes to my cousin, and thanked him for his invitation to visit him at the Palace. I invited him to the White House after the current problems were settled and he accepted. Two helicopters landed on the rear lawn of the Palace and took off. These were decoys. Two more landed, and we got on board for the short flight to Heathrow where Air Force One once again waited for me. We landed and took off in under six minutes as Heathrow was shut down to all air traffic for twenty minutes. We were bound for home with both our support aircraft on our tail as well as three British fighter jets. The U.S. Air Force had orders to meet us half way home, relieve the Brits and escort us into Andrews Air Force Base. I would be relieved once we were back in Washington, even though we had enemies there as well. But at least we were beginning to know who our enemies were.

Thirty miles out from Andrews Air Force Base, I placed a call to the Vice-President as promised. My call was routed to her limousine and when she came on line, I asked rather exasperatedly, "Where the hell are you, you're supposed to be in lock down at the VP residence?"

"At the moment, we just passed through the gates of Andrews and will be waiting on the tarmac to meet you."

"How did you know we were nearing Andrews?"

"David, I *am* the Vice-President after all."

"Okay, well, since you already know, I guess I don't have to tell you. See you on the ground in about fifteen minutes."

I hung up the phone a little hot under the collar because Vicky had failed to follow my directions about remaining locked down for her own safety. Well, at least I can brief her right away, I thought.

"Excuse me, Mr. President – we will be landing in about ten minutes and will be driving to the White House instead of taking Marine One. Secret Service feels it's safer to keep you on the ground," advised Andy Carter.

"Okay, fine, have the VP join me in my limo as she apparently will be on the ground waiting for us."

CHAPTER 13
OPERATION CLEAN SWEEP

T he landing was gentle and we taxied up to hangar one where Air Force One was housed. The door was opened and I bounded down the stairs to salutes from various military personnel as well as a hug from Vicky Wilson. The Secret Service did not want both of us riding in the same limo, but I insisted anyway. In a compromise, I okayed putting the Presidential flag on Limo One, and we rode in an armored backup limousine.

As we sped through the gates and into the early evening, Vicky finally asked, "So, what the hell is going on, David?"

While I filled her in on all the details as we knew them, I could see her eyes widening in the glare of flashing red and blue lights of the motorcade. She found the same things as I did unbelievable.

"What are you going to do about him and the others?"

"I'm going to wait until the FBI and other agencies inform me that they know who all the traitors are. The ones in the Marine Corps have been dealt with already. Until then, we curtail public appearances with the cover that we are working on Middle East policy. What else can we do at this point?"

"Nothing, I guess, except what you suggest. I was told that you increased the detail on my son as well. Is he in any danger?"

"Nothing specific, Vicky, but he is a way to get to you so we must consider him at risk. We need to play it safe. Keep him home from school and out of the public domain. By the way, since you are here, you need to sit in on a meeting I've called in the White House situation room with the military."

Vicky picked up one of the phones in the limo to call the VP residence and spoke to the SAC of her son's detail. She told the agent that no one was permitted access anywhere near her son without her specific okay, and was assured her orders would be implemented at once.

We turned into the White House driveway and entered through a side door. The White House was buzzing like a beehive, not at all what one would expect at this time of day. I was greeted by both Marys, scratching one of them behind the ear, and hugging the other, as well as a relief detail of agents. My regular detail had worked at least forty hours of overtime.

"Welcome home, Mr. President. The Joint Chiefs of Staff are all in the situation room waiting for your arrival."

"Thank you, Mary. I'm going to change first and then go down."

Shane followed me up to the residence, having been first told that the floor was clear by the duty agent. When we walked off of the elevator, I found not the usual one agent, but five in various parts of the entrance hall to the private quarters.

"Shane, where are all these agents coming from? There must be a hundred in the White House right now."

"Sir, under special authority granted to the Director in times of emergency, he can 'borrow' law enforcement agents from other agencies on a temporary basis to fill any need we have. Many of the faces you saw downstairs are from the U.S. Marshal service and Homeland Security. Half of the uniform division is outside patrolling the grounds as well as double duty on the roof of the White House with extra stinger missiles. We are ready for almost anything."

I changed and quickly re-entered my elevator and took it to subbasement three, the home of the situation room. Military guards jumped to attention and saluted at the sight of me as I walked out of the elevator and into the situation room. Inside, the heads of the various military branches stood up to greet me.

"Be seated, gentlemen. First, give me a military update on anything happening anywhere in the world that would concern me."

The Chairman spoke first. "As you ordered, sir, we have begun limited redeployment of combat troops to Afghanistan and started the homeward trip for a few hundred others. The commanders in the field estimate that it will take at least six months to fully comply with your orders so as not to have a chaotic retreat like we saw in Vietnam. So far, six hundred troops have landed in Afghanistan, and two hundred more are on the way home. I know they are small numbers, but it is a start, sir."

"I understand, General, and I don't want a repeat of Vietnam any more than you do. Once again, destroy any equipment deemed not fit for further service and bring out everything else."

"Yes sir, they understand that part of your orders as well."

"Anything else?"

"Sir, we have confirmed that the attack on your hotel was orchestrated by the al-Sadr Brigade. We picked up radio traffic from them claiming a victory for driving you out of Jordan and into Great Britain."

"So, we are now positive that was who was responsible?"

"Yes sir, as much as we can be sure of anything in the Middle East."

"Okay, then this is what I want done. Locate and confirm positive identification on Muqtada al-Sadr. Locate any large grouping of his militia, and locate their headquarters. Once that is done, I want a coordinated hit on all components at once with the goal of killing al-Sadr and as many of his militia as possible while destroying the command structure at their headquarters. Primary goal is to kill al-Sadr as he is a terrorist in command of others. He is no different than Bin Laden as far as I'm concerned. Can the military accomplish this and how soon?"

"Yes, sir, we can get a keyhole satellite over Iraq now, and specifically the city of Al-Najaf where he is headquartered. It will only take about six hours once the order is given."

"Give the order as soon as you have a plan on how to hit all targets at once."

"What about collateral damage, sir, is that a concern?"

"That is a concern, but not big enough to cancel the operation. Why do you ask?"

"Well, one way to hit all targets at once is through the use of Tomahawk missiles launched from a naval ship off the coast. We will pull all of our troops out of Al-Najaf first, and then hit them within a couple of hours. We'll need to leave at least four intelligence agents behind to amend fire coordinates if necessary."

"Admiral, do you have a ship in position that has Tomahawks on board and ready to fire within six hours?"

"Yes, sir, the New Jersey is off shore and could launch and hit targets within five minutes of the go order."

"Gentlemen, give the appropriate orders now."

The commanding officers of the Army, Navy, CIA and a secret organization known only as the 'Intelligence Satellite Group', which controlled Keyhole satellite movements around the world, issued orders to comply with my directive. The operation was in motion.

"General Keens, you are Commandant of the Marine Corps. Bring me up to date on the Marines involved in the plot to assassinate me."

"First of all, I never thought I would hear those words come from the President of the United States. The Corps is devastated over this development. Your orders were complied with and a total of five Marines of various ranks were court martialed, found guilty and sentenced to death. As of an hour ago, none were willing to give up the names of any associates. The order of mandatory review will be on your desk in the morning. You as Commander in Chief review all death sentences passed down by a military court martial."

"What is your recommendation, General? Should I commute the sentences anyway?"

"Sir, they have dishonored their uniforms, the Marine Corps, their country and have betrayed all those who placed their trust in them to protect this nation and to follow the lawful orders of their superiors. It is my view that they deserve no mercy, and I have already signed off on their sentences as Commandant."

"Very well, General, thank you. Let me advise you, I do not hold the Corps in any lesser light as a result of the actions of these cowards and I am still filled with pride in the Marine Corps that you command. If morale is low because of this, schedule an inspection tour of any Marine base in the U.S. as a show of my support, and I will make time to visit the men and women of that base."

"Yes, Mr. President, I think that would be of significant importance and will show them that you still have faith in them. I will schedule it as soon as possible. Camp Lejeune would be the perfect base and is close to Washington."

"Very well, General, make it happen. That's all for now, gentlemen, keep me up to date on this mission."

I left the room with a feeling of pride in the men and women of the armed forces but also with a sense of sorrow that a few rotten apples had affected the morale of the Corps. It must be restored as quickly as possible. As Andy Carter was with me, I told him to get with the General and make the visit happen in the next seven days.

"Andy, get the directors of the CIA and FBI over here for a meeting first thing in the morning. I want an update on the wire taps and proposed action. And now, I'm going to bed."

"Yes, sir."

"Come on, Shane, time to hit the sack, or at least it is for me."

Shane didn't respond; he just smiled. We got off at the residence level and found the number of agents down to only two. I said goodnight to both and headed into my bedroom. As I was closing my door, I heard Shane say goodnight to his buddies also.

I got into bed naked, hoping that my lover would make use of the hidden passage. Two minutes later I heard the bookcase click and then open. Shane came through naked this time, wearing only socks. He left the bookcase open and I asked him why.

"I'd like to sleep in here tonight with you, and should you have a visitor, I want to be able to jet through the bookcase and disappear."

"Lock the door, and get in," I said as I pulled the covers back on the side of the bed that did not have the various phones on the nightstand.

"Shane, I'm really tired tonight, can we just fall asleep in each other's arms instead of one of our crazy-good sex sessions?"

"How about I send you off to sleep with a nice quick blowjob, nothing in return?"

As he fondled my cock, I just smiled and closed my eyes. Far be it for me to turn down a blowjob from a stud like my man Shane. His warm moist mouth brought me off in no time and as he swallowed, there was no cleanup to disturb me. I felt him lie back on the pillows and we fell asleep quickly.

When a knock on my door woke me up at seven A.M., Shane had already left my bed as the bookcase was closed. I got up and put a robe on and answered the door. It was James asking if he should put out my clothes. I opened the door and noticed that Shane was already fully dressed and talking with other agents in the hallway. I followed my usual routine and was in the dining room in forty-five minutes from the time James woke me up, sipping my coffee. Andy Carter joined me, pouring himself coffee and orange juice and sitting down across from me.

"The Directors that you requested will be here in half an hour. May I ask what you intend to do?"

"Yes, you may. If there is sufficient confirmation of the identity of the conspirators, I will request that a Federal arrest warrant be issued today and executed before the sun goes down. Plus, if I'm not mistaken, we are about twenty minutes away from the elimination of some nasty people in Iraq, no?"

"Well actually, no, we are about an hour away from that action taking place. They had trouble locating and verifying al-Sadr's location. Are you sure you want to go through with a public arrest and trial?"

"Well, what alternatives do we have, Andy? Shoot them in the middle of the night, like some third world country?"

"No, of course not. But this is going to shake the country to its very foundation and is going to be a security nightmare keeping them confined until a trial."

"Hmm, you might have a point there. Didn't Gorski push for and orchestrate the imprisonment at Guantanamo Bay in Cuba of anyone associated with terrorists groups? Didn't he fight to keep that base open as a prison under Bush to incarcerate American citizens?"

"Why, yes, he was the darling of the right wing for that achievement. Why?"

"Have an executive order prepared declaring all co-conspirators of the plot to kill me who are working with al-Sadr 'enemy combatants', subject to transportation and imprisonment at Guantanamo. Let's ship the whole nasty bunch down to the Bay. There is a certain poetic justice in that, no?"

"Are you going to run this by the Attorney General?"

"Have him come over after the Directors meeting. I will inform him, but since the Bush administration worked so hard to keep that power in the hands of the President only, I really don't need the AG's okay."

"The shit is going to hit the fan when all this happens."

"Andy, the shit hit the fan in Jordan in case you didn't notice. Make the arrangements for the order."

Mary called up to the residence to advise me that the Directors were in the Oval Office waiting on me.

"Let's go, Shane, time to get moving. Come on, Mary, Daddy needs to work."

"Yes, Mr. President."

As I entered the Oval Office with Andy Carter, the men waiting on me rose to their feet.

"Sit down, gentlemen. Coffee, anyone?" There was a chorus of polite refusals.

"Okay, let's get down to business, then. Where are we on the domestic plot?"

"Sir, we have reconfirmed that one of the voices on the wire tap is without question the Speaker of the House. In subsequent taps, he has been caught again; this time talking about the money he will make working with the Saudis. We believe that he has been in a long term relationship with the Saudi government to create a scheme of kickbacks in exchange for getting approval on the port deal for the Saudis. Pursuant to a court order, we have examined his bank accounts and have found one account that contains more than a million dollars. The transfers were made piecemeal into the account along with several others. All deposits were from electronic overseas origins. Since they came through a Swiss bank, we are unable to determine the original source of the money but we suspect that Saudi Arabia is the starting point."

"Do we have the identities of the other co-conspirators from the wire taps and surveillance?"

"Yes, sir. The others are Jerry McNealy as you already know, Henry Blackwell, President of the Cherbourg Investment firm on Wall Street, Clyde Milkens of Boeing Aircraft, and Robert Brooks, former head of the CIA under Ronald Reagan. The others are employees of the principals. We have photos of them meeting, conversations captured by parabolic mic, and of course wire tap conversations. We have them cold, Mr. President."

"Do you feel we have enough for warrants?"

"Yes, sir. We can charge them with treason along with a host of other charges," replied the FBI Director.

"Do you have a judge who will issue all warrants today?"

"We have Judge Sandra Wilcox on standby. She has no idea for what, but she agreed to be available to us today."

"How long will it take to prepare the probable cause statements for the warrants, and get them to the Court?"

"We can probably be in front of Judge Wilcox by three this afternoon."

"Any indication that any other members of Congress are involved in this?"

"No, sir. We have been able to identify only the Speaker."

"Very well, get the warrants, and arrest them today if you can. Make Gorski the first one arrested."

"MARY, do you have that order ready for signature?"

The door to the Oval Office opened and Mary came in with one of her now famous blue folders with the Presidential seal on it. I opened it and read Executive Order number 67. It authorized the detention of all those involved in the plot to be incarcerated at Guantanamo Bay. I signed it as well as a copy.

"Gentlemen, this is an Executive Order I just signed mandating those who will be arrested today be transported to GitMo where they will be held until further action. I have declared them 'enemy combatants' under the authority that George Bush managed to squeeze out of Congress. Therefore, once arrested, have them taken there pronto. Any questions?"

"I'll need a copy of the Executive Order authorizing this," said the Director of the FBI.

I handed the copy to him, and told them to get moving on the arrests. "This will be called 'Operation Clean Sweep'."

As they got up to leave, the phone rang and I was told that the Chairman of the Joints Chiefs was waiting to see me.

As the current group of men left, the General entered.

"Mr. President, the orders that you gave concerning al-Sadr and the other targets have been successfully carried out. All targets have been destroyed as ordered."

"Outstanding, General, my compliments to the men involved in this operation. Did we suffer any casualties?"

"None have been reported. We are presently engaged in the process of extracting the intelligence operatives who remained behind with the targets."

"Very well, General, thank you for this good news. General, I would like the Pentagon to hold a press conference announcing this as military targets taken out."

"Yes, Mr. President."

The General left and I sat down at my desk, contemplating the actions I had been forced to take in a matter of days since becoming President. This wasn't what I had planned for the opening days of my Administration, but history and events beyond my control forced my hand.

I asked Shane to come into my office and sit down.

"Look, Shane, I'm telling you this, but I do not want the rest of the Secret Service to know for a couple of reasons. Later today there will be a series of arrests that will include the Speaker of the House and some VIP industry types who will then be shipped off to GitMo. The arrests are going to stir up a lot of trouble and I want you to be ready. Once the arrests are accomplished, the Secret Service should be fully advised. But I don't want the targets tipped off early because of a leak in the Secret Service."

"Holy shit, Guantanamo Bay? That is going to hit the fan."

"Well, if the Republican Congress doesn't like their Speaker being sent away to the Cuban Med, then they can repeal the law that gave Bush the authority to do exactly this any time he felt like it. It's one way to start repealing the abuses of authority committed by Bush and his cronies."

"This is going to shock a lot of people."

"Well, that's why I'm telling you now. You'd better buckle your seatbelt, because it's going to be a bumpy ride."

At 4:45 in the afternoon, six FBI agents entered the office of the Speaker of the House and forced their way into a meeting where Speaker Gorski was talking about defense issues.

"FBI, everyone stay as you are!"

"What in the hell is the meaning of this, are you people crazy? Do you know who I am?"

"Sir, who exactly are you?" asked the lead agent.

"Why, I'm Speaker Gorski and you are interrupting a meeting!"

"Great, now that we've confirmed your identity from your own mouth, you, sir, are under arrest."

Three agents moved behind the desk and lifted the Speaker out of his chair and placed him in handcuffs just as Capitol Hill police arrived en mass at the door with guns drawn.

"Police! Release the Speaker now!" commanded a police Lieutenant.

"FBI! We have a Federal warrant to arrest Speaker Gorski, now stand down and cease your obstruction of Federal agents carrying out an order from the Court!"

The FBI agent in charge walked over to the police Lieutenant and showed him the arrest warrant. He looked it over and then told his men to holster their weapons and let the agents through with the Speaker.

"What am I being charged with?" the Speaker demanded to know.

"Treason as well as other charges, now let's go."

The FBI rushed Gorski out of the hallways of Congress, past a couple of members of the Press who were startled to see the Speaker in handcuffs, and into waiting cars which sped away – not to the Federal

Courthouse as would be normal, but to Andrews Air Force Base, where he was loaded onto a plane that took off for Cuba.

At that same exact moment, five other teams of FBI agents arrested their targets and transported them to military bases for confinement until they could be sent to Cuba. In a matter of twenty minutes, all known conspirators were under arrest and being transported to the American Gulag system created by Bush and Cheney.

News broke of the arrests at 5:35, just in time for the six o'clock evening news, with few details and wild speculation. I left it to the FBI to explain what had happened and why. The biggest point of interest was the fact that the defendants were placed into military custody and not the criminal justice system. The White House switchboard was flooded with calls from angry people wanting to know why Gorski and company were on their way to Cuba.

At precisely 6:37 P.M., I went on national television during the evening news to answer questions. After detailing the involvement of the defendants, I was asked how I could possibly send American citizens to GitMo.

"The Republican Congress passed and George Bush signed legislation that allowed an American president to do what I have done today. The defendants were working with foreign powers, to wit: the Saudi Arabian government, and terrorist groups in Iraq. Their aim was to bring down the present Administration, which was to include Vice-President Wilson, clearing the way for Speaker Gorski to become President. This would have effectively shifted the White House back into Republican control, and enabled the rest of the plot to take effect. Vast amounts of money would have been funneled into the pockets of some very rich men in exchange for selling our ports to the Saudis, as well as giving control up of some of our military capability, thus playing into the hands of the enemy."

"Mr. President, there are loud calls for you to bring back to American soil all of the men charged today and put them into the criminal justice system. How do you respond to those demands?"

"Well, if Congress doesn't like how this President exercised their law, then they need to repeal the law and send it to my desk for signature. They created this monster, they can kill it. Congress must remember that when they pass such legislation to appease the current occupant of the White House, they are giving all future Presidents the same power. It appears this law should have never been enacted or proposed in the first place."

"Mr. President, is this it? Has the plot to bring you down failed and is it now over?"

"All I can say is that the current plot is finished. If the Congress will get on board with reforms that are badly needed as a direct result of the abuse of power in this city over the past eight years, then maybe yes, the coup d'état is over. You see, the fact that I am a gay American was never the real reason behind the attempts on my life. It was greed, both political and monetary, that led this group of desperate men on the path to perdition. I wish to give my profound thanks and respect to the following Federal Agencies for their diligence and tenacity in stopping these men: the FBI, the CIA, the Secret Service, the NSA, and the military. With brave men and women such as these, America will always survive the forces of evil that attempt to subvert the will of the people. I have no further comments at this time, thank you."

En route back to my office, I ran into the Commandant of the Marine Corps in one of the hallways.

"Good evening, Mr. President."

"Good evening, General. Now that this business is behind us for the time being, would you arrange for a visit to Camp Lejeune within the next couple of days? I want to attend to that morale problem as soon as possible. In fact, make it an overnight trip, I'll stay on base and that will count as my base inspection for the Marines."

"Yes, sir, of course. I will alert the base and let your Chief of Staff know the exact days. The Marines at Lejeune will be honored to have you visit, sir."

"Great, I look forward to it, General."

When I turned towards the residence elevator instead of the hallway leading to the Oval Office, I heard Shane mumble, "Thank God, I'm beat." When it was just the two of us alone on the elevator, Shane spoke up.

"God almighty, you mean I've got to worry about you on a base surrounded by a thousand or so young Marines? Look what happened when just one cute one got near you!"

"Well, Agent Thompson, as soon as I have a ring on my finger, you'll never have to worry about any man in a uniform again!"

John Simpson, a Vietnam era Veteran, has been a uniformed Police Officer of the year, a Federal Agent, a Federal Magistrate, an armed bodyguard to royalty and a senior Government executive, with awards from the Vice-President of the United States and the Secretary of the Treasury. John now writes and is the author of "Murder Most Gay," a full-length novel, with a sequel entitled "Task Force," both coming out through Dreamspinner Press, and numerous short stories for Alyson Books. Additionally, he has written articles for various gay and straight magazines. John lives with his partner of 35 years and three wonderful Scott Terriers, all spoiled. John is also involved with the Old Catholic Church and its liberal pastoral positions on the Gay community.

Visit John's Website at www.johnsimpsonbooks.com

Novels from Dreamspinner Press

Alliance in Blood by Ariel Tachna   232 pages
Paperback $11.99   eBook $5.99
ISBN: 978-0-9815084-9-8   **ISBN**: 978-0-9817372-1-8

Can a desperate wizard and a bitter, disillusioned vampire find a way to build the partnership that could save their world?

In a world rocked by magical war, vampires are seen by many as less than human, as the stereotypical creatures of the night who prey on others. But as the war intensifies, the wizards know they need an advantage to turn the tide in their favor: the strength and edge the vampires can give them in the battle against the dark wizards who seek to destroy life as they know it.

In a dangerous move and show of good will, the wizards ask the leader of the vampires to meet with them, so that they might plead their cause. One desperate man, Alain Magnier, and one bitter, disillusioned vampire, Orlando St. Clair, meet in Paris, and the fate of the world hangs in the balance of their decision: Will the vampires join the cause and form a partnership with the wizards to win the war?

The first of a four part series.

The Archer by Abigail Roux   576 pages
Paperback $19.99   eBook $8.99
ISBN: 978-0-9815084-8-1   **ISBN**: 978-0-9817372-0-1

Rocked to the core by traitors and spies, the Organization made an unprecedented move in bringing together six highly trained men to track down one rogue wolf: The Archer.

There are three field agents: one at the top of his game, one hoping to retire, and another walking the line; a cold-blooded assassin who can use any weapon known to man; a demolitions expert who can't resist the allure of fire; and a computer hacker with more tricks in his mouse than Houdini. This team is made up of the best of the best, and if it can't succeed in this impossible mission, no one can. But no plan survives first contact with the enemy – especially when you can't even find out who he is!

Despite what a cluster the assignment is from the start, the six men try to get their act together to track down the rogue operative, and in the process they discover there's more to life than the next assignment. Now it's up to them to survive by working together and determining who the real traitor is: an unknown friend, a close-by enemy, or the Organization itself.

Order on-line at www.dreamspinnerpress.com

Caught Running by Urban & Roux   236 pages
Paperback $11.99   **eBook** $5.99
ISBN: 978-0-9801018-8-1   **ISBN**: 978-0-9801018-9-8

Ten years after graduation, Jake "the jock" Campbell and Brandon "the nerd" Bartlett are teaching at their old high school and still living in separate worlds. When Brandon is thrown into a coaching job on Jake's baseball team, they find themselves learning more about each other than they'd ever expected. High school is all about image – even for the teachers. Brandon and Jake have to get past their preconceived notions to find the friendship needed to work together. And somewhere along the way, they discover that perceptions can always change for the better.

Cursed by Rhianne Aile   232 pages
Paperback $11.99   **eBook** $5.99
ISBN: 978-0-9795048-2-2   **ISBN**: 978-0-9795048-3-9

Upon their grandmother's death, Tristan Northland and his twin, Will, come into possession of her Book of Shadows and the knowledge that their family is responsible for a centuries old curse. Determined to right the ancient wrong, Tristan sets off across the ocean to reverse the dark magic that affects the Sterling family to this day.

Benjamin Sterling might not be happy with his life, but it is predictable – at least until Tristan Northland shows up in his office, unannounced and with nowhere to stay. He has plenty of reason to distrust witches and Northlands, but instead of caution, he experiences two unexpected emotions: hope and love

Diplomacy by Zahra Owens   228 pages
Paperback $11.99   **eBook** $5.99
ISBN: 978-0-9801018-6-7   **ISBN**: 978-0-9801018-9-8

Jack Christensen has everything he ever wanted. He's a rising star in US Diplomacy, the youngest man to have been appointed as an Ambassador of the United States. A career diplomat who's just been sent to a politically interesting Embassy in Europe, he has the perfect wife, speaks five languages and has all the right credentials, yet there's something missing and he doesn't quite know what.

Then Lucas Carlton walks into an Embassy reception and introduces himself and his American fiancée. From the first handshake, the young Englishman makes an impression on Jack that leaves him confused and uncharacteristically insecure. Lucas' position as the British liaison to the American Embassy means they are forced to work together closely and they have a hard time denying the attraction between them, despite their current relationships.

Diplomatic circles are notoriously conservative though, and they each know that the right woman by their side makes a very significant contribution to their success. Will they be able to make the right choices in their professional and personal lives? Or will they need to sacrifice one for the other?

Gold Warrior by Clare London   240 pages
Paperback $11.99   **eBook** $5.99
ISBN: 978-0-9815084-4-3   **ISBN**: 978-0-9815084-5-0

Maen is a Gold Warrior, a defender of Aza City, a world controlled by the Queen and her womankind where the best of men are maintained for the military and the women's pleasure. A favorite of his imperious Mistress and a leader among his men, Maen is too cautious to seek casual sexual satisfaction and so stays alone, taking his comfort in ensuring a stable and controlled world. That world is thrown into disarray by Dax, a bold and challenging new Bronze soldier who excites Maen with his fierce hero worship and leads them to a forbidden affair. They find themselves thrown together in a dangerous and hostile environment without the support of the City and far away from their loyalties, and Maen finds himself risking everything for Dax – his position; his loyalties; and eventually, his life.

Order on-line at www.dreamspinnerpress.com

Love Ahead by Urban & Roux   308 pages
Paperback $14.99   **eBook** $6.99
ISBN: 978-0-9817372-4-9   **ISBN**: 978-0-9817372-5-6

A pair of working man novellas.

Under Contract

Site foreman Ted Lucas moved to Birmingham, leaving a full life behind, only to discover something - someone - to look forward to. Assistant Nick Cooper catches his eye, and even more incredibly, Lucas's heart, all without a word. When Lucas finds out Cooper's asked to be transferred, he bites the bullet and admits his feelings. Intrigued, Cooper offers Lucas one night to figure out if that love could possibly be real.

Over the Road

Truck driver Elliot Cochran meets 'McLean' while talking on the CB and strikes up an unusual friendship. One evening, McLean tells Elliot he needs to go find some companionship, and so Elliot meets Jimmy Vaughan - and has one of the best nights in his life. Before long Elliot faces a decision about sharing his life: Does he choose McLean, the best friend he's never met, or Jimmy, the man who thrills him beyond belief.

Murder Most Gay by John Simpson   220 pages
Paperback $11.99   **eBook** $5.99
ISBN: 978-0-9817372-2-5   **ISBN**: 978-0-9817372-3-2

A serial killer is targeting gay men, preying on them in popular bars and parks. Assigned to the case, rookie cop Pat St. James feels all too close to the victims. He's gay and firmly in the closet at work. The fact that he's sent undercover as a gay man is a stroke of irony.

Pat and his fellow cop, Hank, are hanging out in bars, trying to get a lead on the killer. At the same time, Pat's looking for Mr. Right – juggling three men, hoping he'll find the perfect match for himself. He picked up Bill at a bar, Dean's a longtime friend … and in yet another ironic twist, his partner, Hank, is also gay and on the list of possible beaus.

As the killer continues to rampage, strangling and raping his victims, Pat has to focus on his work and hope that his personal life survives the stress. But when his hopes and dreams for happiness overlap with the investigation, Pat may be headed for big trouble.

Order on-line at www.dreamspinnerpress.com

A Summer Place by Ariel Tachna 248 pages
Paperback $11.99   **eBook** $5.99
ISBN: 978-0-9795048-4-6   ISBN: 978-0-9795048-5-3

Overseer Nicolas Wells had been coming to Mount Desert Island for ten summers to help build cottages for the rich and powerful. Despite his secrets, he had grown comfortable in the peaceful little island town, getting to know its inhabitants and even to consider some of them friends. The eleventh year, however, he arrived to startling news: the island's peace had been shattered by a murder. At the request of the sheriff, Shawn Parnell, Nicolas agreed to hire Philip Hall, the local blacksmith and the probable next victim, in the hope that the secure construction site would be safer than his house in the village. He never expected the decision to lead to danger. Or to love.

To Love a Cowboy by Rhianne Aile 228 pages
Paperback $11.99   **eBook** $5.99
ISBN: 978-0-9795048-8-4   ISBN: 978-0-9795048-9-1

Seven years ago, Roan Bucklin left the family ranch for college, leaving foreman Patrick Lassiter with a mix of sweltering emotions: relief, regret, and nearly overwhelming desire. Afraid that Roan would regret giving himself to an older man, Patrick let him go without a word about his true feelings. But Roan took Patrick's heart with him.

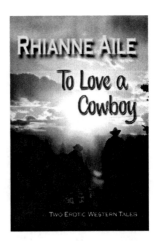

Roan had harbored a crush on Patrick from the time he'd turned fourteen. He thought he'd gotten over it, grown up, moved on, but now he's back and home to stay. After one look, he knows he has something to prove to Patrick – that he wants to be claimed by the cowboy who has always possessed his heart.

Twisted Brand by Clare London   288 pages
Paperback $14.99   **eBook** $6.99
ISBN: 978-0-9817372-6-3   **ISBN**: 978-0-9817372-7-0

Sequel to <u>*The Gold Warrior*</u>

No longer a revered Gold Warrior, Maen is a disgraced soldier, held in suspicion despite his role in winning the Queenship of Aza City for his Mistress, Seleste. Returned alive from his captivity by the rebel Exiles, his reward was to be cast out from his position, his brave loyalty dismissed. He remains an unwilling thrall to the new Queen while his heart mourns the memory of Dax, the young Bronzeman he helped escape from a sentence of death.

When Maen is put under the guard of the arrogant Gold Warrior Zander and given the thankless task of preparing a Royal History, they both join up with the lively scribe Kiel. The youngster's bold curiosity initiates a chain of events that will change their world and that of the City forever. Maen's own discoveries will cast a new and shocking light on the Royal history and stir revolution in both citizens and rebels. And he will finally return to the Exile camp to face the one thing that can make him choose desire over duty.

Order on-line at www.dreamspinnerpress.com

Printed in the United States
122892LV00004B/112-147/P